1000 WORDS

'Stick to the story, will you please,' quips my wife, Bella, as she unloads the grocery bags onto the breakfast bar bench. 'Do not wander off, and for goodness' sake, keep it under 1,000 words.'

My mind is like a precision missile when sharing a topic or a story, but my tongue often takes the scenic route. So, I ask the reader to be patient with me.

I am sitting at the breakfast bar of our vacation home on Minnow Island telling this story. You know the island I am speaking of, I am sure. It is the one of the New South Wales (NSW) coastline, but not the island where Gilligan and his boat got stranded (see, there I go again). Anyway, I tell the missus that my seventeen-year-old daughter and I have taken a walk near the shore on our private beach this morning. Yes, you read right, our private beach.

Little over 100 years ago, my grandfather had the foresight (others at the time said he was plum loco) to purchase this island of 1 ½ hectares, which is about twenty-one kilometres from Rose Bay NSW. While twenty-one kilometres offshore, we still have a Rose Bay postcode since we use the local post office, so it is a lot easier to say we have a vacation home in Rose Bay, rather tn Minnow Island.

To continue with my story, I tell my wife that we see a lump of blackness on the pristine sand as we are walking on the beach. We can not miss it. My daughter and I get closer to the still lump. It seems to be a small, and it appears incredibly ragged. Skeletal would be a better description. It is lying on its side and barely breathing. Mary Lou (that's my daughter's name, in case I have not mentioned it) looks at the animal and breaks down crying, saying, 'Save it, Papi, save it.'

What can I do?

I remove my t-shirt, pick it up lean and wrap the poor animal with it and softly cradle the fragile animal, noticing a lack of a tail as if a boat propeller had chopped it off. We rush back to the house to provide what medical help I can afford (which is consistent with wrapping my t-shirt around the poor thing, since I have no veterinarian skills to speak of).

We give the animal some water to which he or she (I have not looked underneath, thinking that some privacy is the etiquette at this moment) to which it responds in sheer delight. I notice that the little thing, well, is not so small after all. The cat has a thick and blunt nose, small eyes, small ears and a long body. With short hair, and, even in a skeletal form, the cat probably comes in at around 2 kilos in weight and is close to 90 cm long. We give it some nuts

STORIES TO SHARE WITH MY PARTNER
BOOK 1

A BOOK OF STORIES TO ENJOY TOGETHER!

STORIES TO SHARE WITH MY PARTNER–BOOK 1

STORIES TO SHARE WITH MY PARTNER–BOOK 1

Nodar, José F.

ISBN [978-0-6452639-0-9] (print)

ISBN: [978-0-6452639-2-3] (Kindle)

ISBN [978-0-6452639-1-6] (large print)

ISBN: [978-0-6452639-3-0] (E-pub)

ISBN [978-0-6452639-4-7] (audiobook)

ABOUT THIS BOOK

This book is an anthology of fictional short stories and possibly also a few poems. Most of these stories are an accumulation of yarns I wrote while participating in a writers' group in Camden, New South Wales, either in our spontaneous writing sessions or as 'homework.'

There is no rhyme, reason or purpose to the stories other than to, hopefully, make you smile and enjoy them while doing your thing on the toilet.

They are short, with each story taking less than four-minutes to read. So, in-and-out, I say, and off to do other things.

ACKNOWLEDGEMENTS

Foremost, I wish to acknowledge the spiritual and moral support I received from my wife.

I dedicate this book to you, Red!

Without this support, and the many breakfasts, lunches and dinners she has cooked for me in our twenty-odd years of marriage together, I would not have the strength to sit in front of a screen and pound the keys.

Second, a big thank you to the writing group members, my companions in the writing trenches who have given me instruction and courage to put pen to paper and help me through the years.

TABLE OF CONTENTS

and a bit of grain cereal, and the darling cat seems to perk up out of its zombie like state. We can appreciate how happy and grateful he or she is becoming.

The days go by, and even my wife is getting used to the little thing which I name Robinson (yes, we found out that it was a male). It loves to play with us, jumping on us as we sit on our sofa enjoying beautiful sunsets as we sip our Hunter Valley delicious red wines.

As our time in vacationland is ending, Mary Lou declares Robinson should take the trip back home with us. Of course, I am hesitant but agree to the idea only if we take Robinson to a vet before our trip back to Sydney (which will be a challenge with the cat in the SUV). We decide to take Robinson to see Dr. James Kildare, who has an office next to the *Hilltop Cottage*. Yes, he has the same name as the TV character Dr. Kildare, played by Richard Chamberlain, who worked with Lee Kurty, who played Nurse Zoe Lawton, in the TV series. However, our doctor has no nurse like Zoe.

Darn it, stop it; there I go again!

The visit to see Dr. Kildare is a success.

Robinson clears all known tests to determine that he is in excellent health and ready for the long road trip back home. Dr. Kildare asks for Mary Lou to step outside so that he could speak with me in private. He assures Mary Lou that Robinson is fine and that he just wants a few minutes with me to discuss payment for the visit. Mary Lou and Robinson step out of the examination room, and Dr. Kildare shares his thoughts with me.

On the day of our planned returned trip to Sydney, Robinson seems to have disappeared. We look high and low, but there is no sign of Robinson. Mary Lou is inconsolable and refuses to leave unless we find him. After much consoling, Mary Lou accepts our explanations that Robinson did not want to leave his familiar surroundings and not to hurt her feelings, he just slipped away during the night. I make a new promise that once we arrive in Sydney, we would do a quick run to the animal shelter to satisfy Mary Lou's desire for a new 'Robinson.' The suggestion for a new 'Robinson' was all we needed for the road trip back to Sydney.

Time passes, and Mary Lou graduates from the University of New South Wales. As she prepares to head off to Chicago, USA, for her new job, Bella says to me, 'I am surprised that you did not faint when Dr. Kildare told you that Robinson was not a cat, but a Gambian pouched rat.'

No, I can proudly say I did not faint. I can say I was conniving enough to get rid of the Gambian pouched rat and end up telling the reader this whopper of a story in less than 1000 words.

A SUMPTUOUS DINNER

As snow falls and blankets our front yard, I sit in my office watching the park across the street. It is filled with children of all ages, playing and enjoying the brisk winter breeze on their rosy cheeks.

My wife, Bella, is in the kitchen labouring in the act of love that she performs every day, 364 days a year, and this one additional day, the 365th. It is the most special of all — *Noche Buena*.

Noche Buena (Good Night) is the Spanish word for Christmas Eve. In Spain, Latin America and the Philippines, the evening comprises a traditional family dinner. Roasted pig or lechón is often the focus of Noche Buena for feasts around the world.

My wife makes 'Noche Buena' as Cuban as you can get, but she has now had to incorporate four additional nationalities into the mix as our family has grown and extended over the years.

Caribbean flavours rise from the various pots, cooking the black beans, yellow rice and yuca that bring back my childhood memories of many years ago.

As I baste the lechón with a mixture of garlic, salt, black pepper, cumin, oregano and coriander, it already fills the kitchen with a fantastic aromatic smell.

A potpourri of pot roast with creamy mushroom grits and sweet potato souffle conjures up that sweet Southern feeling for my American daughter and two grandchildren born in Miami, Florida.

We can already start feeling our lips flapping as the grits stir in the pot with the mushrooms.

Now the oven will be shared by the lechón and the rest of the Australian components of this meal–the ham and the turkey–making it the trifecta of food.

Of course, final nationality dish is up. A large dish of Maltese 'timpana' that every Maltese mother has learned to cook, passed her own recipe through generations in this tiny island paradise.

Add to this the pre-meal obligatory serving of Australian king prawns, and we have the overwhelming feeling that Noche Buena is here and is ready to take off in our family home.

We sit around the large dining room table. All the food is now in front of our hungry eyes and the proud smiles of my great chef-wife, who again has superseded all of our expectations.

We notice that the evening has descended on us. Through the porch lights, we see the snow falling and creating small mounds on the frosty ground and the snow also sprinkles itself on the bare tree branches. This cosy feeling allows us to enjoy the meal along with some great Australian wine and Spanish cider, making all this comfort food even more delightful to enjoy and share.

The wife knows how to make these crowd-pleasers so delightful to enjoy and servings that are of most minimal clean-up effort so even the grandchildren can pick up and clear the table.

The older males become useless because of the liquor, and the tryptophan from the turkey all consume on an empty stomach, thus incapacitating these husky, brawny male specimens. They become silly, sleepy gnomes who must unbuckle their pants while sitting on the family room sofa and recliners.

When the men wake up, we sit around the open-fire chimney sipping a glass of sherry, again another delicacy from Spain, but with the name like Harvey Bristol cream, you would not believe it comes from Spain.

We all smile and agree. We had a sumptuous dinner.

A WIN-WIN

Mabel's Pancake House is legendary in downtown Centerville, Georgia. You might wonder what Centreville is famous for, besides Mabel's Pancake House.

Well, while he explored Georgia, Hernando de Soto passed through what it is now known as Centreville, an area crossing the Quechan River and the present-day eastern boundary line of the city limits. A historical marker on the courthouse grounds commemorates his visit. The Wilcox County courthouse itself, built in 1903, is listed on the National Register of Historic Places.

Centreville, famous for its large population of wild hogs, is nicknamed 'Wild Hog Capital of Georgia'. It holds the annual Centreville Wild Hog Festival in May, with food, arts, and crafts, live music and various contests.

One of these contests is the high-noon pancake eating contest at Mabel's.

That is how I wound up in jail.

The local town paper, the *Centreville Voice*, has in me in the front page displayed as 'local-boy-gone-bad.' Goodness me, why did they say that?

My day started as your day probably starts.

My usual cheerful disposition was in place as I ran through my morning routine of showering and shaving. I read the *Centreville Voice* with my cup of coffee on my front porch, while watching folks getting ready for their daily chores.

As the retired police sheriff of Centreville (which has a population 2,908, not counting the wild hogs), the populace had been good to me.

After 34 years of being elected to this position, I keep just about everyone happy and our crimes have never risen higher than vandalism - like the day Billy Joe Royal sprayed painted on old man Butler's car with shaving cream. 'Why?' you ask. Simply because Billy Joe believes in the Halloween saying of 'trick or treat' and since Billy Joe got no treats, old man Butler got his trick.

As I savour my coffee, I read that the annual Centreville Wild Hog Festival is coming up. Mabel's pancakes are world-renowned (with the 'world' here, defined as no further than the *Hoglet Supermarket* on West Main Street and the *Low Pharmacy* on East Main Street). If you pass either of these located fixtures in Centreville, well, you missed Centreville.

My old office, on East Main Street, between Cemetery Road and Prison Road (which of course leads you to the Centreville Correctional Facility, hence the name of the road) makes it easy for folks to find, but I digress.

Getting back to Mabel's pancakes… I have never taken part in the annual contest, but I know it is fun from being a judge a few times in the past. So, I thought that this year it might just behoove me to join in. The prize is one year's breakfast at Mabel's (understanding that you can only eat up to $8.99–including tax–so as not to break the bank for Mabel). Just common courtesy, you know.

The contest is easy. Eat as many pancakes as you can in 10 minutes–not stopping to wash it down with milk, coffee, water or any other type of liquid. Maple syrup will accompany the flapjacks. You may add as much maple syrup as you want, and butter galore if you wish, and if you are one of those fancy-dandies, cream.

Being a widower, I figure that a free breakfast for the next 365 days would make for an excellent way to start the day, meet my old constituents, and give me a reason to jolt myself out of bed. Besides, I could also save money by cancelling my subscription to the *Centreville Voice*, since Mabel has several copies delivered to her each day — Sunday through Saturday.

So, I check the date for the contest and find that I only have eight days to wait until the big day. I start my regime of adapting my pace to breakfast by not eating as much the previous evening, and nothing but my cup of coffee in the morning. The strategy I have adopted makes every day feel that I am getting more onerous.

This strategy delivers the expected results since, by the morning of the contest, I am famished and could have eaten one wild hog if it wandered on my front lawn. No, I think I could have eaten two of the wild hogs if they wandered in.

As I arrive at Mabel's, I notice the competition.

Last year's winner, Bobby Ray Millan, is there. He is all smiles, thinking that he will again have free breakfast for another year.

Sherman Wilcox, the local barber, is also taking part, but no way he can win — his girth is already at the maximum point. He could only just fit through Mabel's front door.

Shirley Williamson, the high school English teacher, has joined in this year after the encouragement of the entire football team. You know, she might have a chance because she is as skinny as a rail–she must stand up twice to make a shadow. That might be enough to make her a contender.

Then, of course, the deputy sheriff of Centreville, Jimmy Tate Patrick, born and raised in Centreville. Darn, I knew his pappy since we went to the local high school, way back when, so I figure he is also another good contender.

There are three judges this year as always.

Miss Mabel, of course, is always a judge. So is the honourable Judge Darius Lee Rocker. He has always been a pain in my rear end since he is a stickler for the fine points of the law, whereas I am a bit more, let's say, discrete, in handling issues of the city. Then there is the new sheriff, Garland Heywood Kemper, a transplant city slicker from Atlanta, that applied for the position and got the job anyway, since he is a friend of the judge.

So, at noon, we are sitting on one sizeable, long bench, with only a fork, a knife, and plenty of maple syrup and butter. We can smell the pancakes and see Reba Scarlet Walden cooking enough pancakes to feed both the entire high school football team and the whole of Centreville Baptist church congregation.

Judge Kemper lowers the flag, and the race starts.

My strategy is simple, loosen my belt and begin eating.

Pancakes, syrup, pancakes, butter, pancakes, butter and syrup. I run a mixture of this pattern, not to count, but to eat and eat until the prize is mine. I can feel it in my stomach (sorry for the pun).

Never looking at the wall clock, before I know it, Judge Kemper yells 'Stop! Forks down!' The fastest ten minutes of my life have gone by, so I straighten my shirt a bit, tuck it in, and buckle my belt once again. I am expecting my name will herald me as the winner, and I can collect my prize.

You might imagine I have lost count of the number of pancakes I had eaten. I did, but I just knew that I had won.

The three judges confer for what seems like an eternity and come back with a verdict - Jimmy Tate Patrick is the winner.

Well, I feel robbed for sure.

I get up to demand a recount, not noticing that the tablecloth has become entwined with my belt. The entire table of pancakes, maple syrup and butter spill on the three judges, making Garland Heywood Kemper one unhappy sheriff.

He is so unhappy that he handcuffs me and takes me to the courthouse, where Judge Darius Lee Rocker slaps a 30-day sentence on me for creating a public nuisance.

Well, I did not win the Centreville Wild Hog Festival pancake contest or a year's worth of free breakfast, but I got 30-days' worth of meals at the Centreville Correctional Facility. So — a win-win, wouldn't you say?

ALONE

They said it could not happen.

They prophesied the Apocalypse, and they did not believe it.

Oh, they said the End-of-Days was coming, but they did not accept its truth.

Then it happened.

It took everything from Mary in an instantaneous flash. She saw the giant mushroom, and she knew it was going to be the end of everything.

There would be no future for her. She was alone, she knew. The last of her kind that survived the human-made mushroom that rained from the sky on her land.

Everything she had, her parents, her husband, her children, her people, her future — her future — all gone in that flash, as if they had not even been born.

She knew that there could be no survivors, and she knew — she was now forever alone.

Mary sat in the darkness of her home, as if floating on a dark sea with only the stars to be seen through her front porch window, alone.

One way she filled her days was with tasks around the little shack she built, keeping busy, her mind occupied. But when the nights arrived... The nights were worse.

Alone.

Summers were also terrible, but she could at least sit by the river that ran along her little shack and watch the currents bring her a small smile now and then. But when the winters arrived, and the river froze... The nights, they were worse.

Alone is all Mary could think. She was alone. Nothing could have survived the blast.

But then there was a knock on her front door.....

CHARLOTTE

My sweet neighbour of a few months, Ms. Jo, had made a major decision in her life. She had decided it was time to move—downsize to be exact—and to sell most of her knick-knacks, trinkets, curios and other articles she had collected over the years.

My first encounter with Ms. Jo was when I moved in next to her, and she invited me for tea and scones. She was such a lovely, elegant lady, so I accepted, knowing in advance from the neighbours across the street that she was an excellent pastry cook. They had also told me she could be quirky. How much of a quirk, however, I did not realise until I walked into her parlour and saw at least 1,000 dolls of all sizes, fashions, textures and styles.

As we sat in her parlour, Ms. Jo told me stories about the dolls. When she bought them, who gave her which one and, of course, her favourite—Charlotte.

'When I found her at the local op-shop, she wore a beautiful frock with a lace-up bodice, a pretty petticoat and knee-length lace trimmed panties. She even had a smart pair of cream and fawn lace-up boots,' said Ms. Jo.

'She was a bargain,' Ms. Jo exclaimed. 'I got her for $10.50 at the local op-shop, and she has been my favourite ever since.'

Ms. Jo continued her litany of love towards the doll, saying that she placed Charlotte on a little bedroom chair in her room, looking all tranquil and sad, even wishing Charlotte were alive so she could speak with her.

It was a lovely story, which I enjoyed even more than I partook of my third, or was it my fourth, scone?

Then Ms Jo dropped a bombshell. 'I will sell all the dolls in the coming weeks, but I want you to have Charlotte. I know she will be an amazing companion to you.'

First, I was astounded, but then I felt a warm feeling knowing that this treasure Ms. Jo thought so much of would be mine, and I felt honoured. So, I accepted. I took Charlotte into my arms and brought her into the bosom of my home.

It only took four weeks for Ms. Jo to sell all her knick-knacks, trinkets, curios and other articles she had collected over the years, as well as all her dolls. Add another week, and she had sold her home. Add another month, and I stood on my front porch waving to Ms. Jo as she left her home on fresh adventures, as she called it.

A few days passed, and I thought of the times I used to see old Ms. Jo watering her flowers or running after her old cat, Beauty, who ran out the front door every time she could. Scared by ghosts, I thought, and smiled to myself. In the end, Beauty was always found and brought back in the cradled arms of Ms. Jo into her home.

A few more weeks passed, and the darndest things happened. While watching TV downstairs, I would hear voices emitting from my bedroom upstairs. I never had more than one TV on at a time, and I seldom forgot to turn one off or the other on, so I was in bewilderment as to the whereabouts of the voices.

Every time I heard them, I was downstairs, but when I went upstairs and entered my bedroom, no voices were to be heard. No TV on, nor the radio. All you would find was Charlotte, sitting on the divan next to my bed, where Ms. Jo suggested I place the doll.

Over time I gave up investigating the voices, but then, even stranger things happened.

As I slept late into the evening, the same voices would awaken me. But as soon as I opened my eyes and turned on the nightstand light, there was nothing. The TV was not on, the radio was not on, and I never brought my mobile phone into the room. So, it could not have been someone calling and the message going into voicemail.

Strange.

These occurrences went on for a few months until I heard the voices, turned the nightstand light on and - do not think I had been drinking that night–but I could swear that Charlotte had moved from the divan to the chair next to my bed.

Now, it was possible that the last time I watched TV on the divan, I might have moved the doll into the chair, and just forgotten to place it back.

Yes, that had to be it.

I put her back on the divan and went back to sleep.

A few hours passed, and again voices startled and woke me. This time I turned the lights on again quickly, and noticed Charlotte was not on the divan but in the chair next to my bed.

Now, I am not a believer in ghosts or being possessed, but I remembered taking the doll from the chair and placing it on the divan, turning off the lights, and going to bed.

I repeated the process and tried to catch a few more minutes of shut eye before dawn. Just before dawn, voices streamed into my ears–so close, as if whispered–and I turned to find Charlotte in the bed with me. As I jumped out of bed, the bejeezus scared out of me. I thought I saw a smile on the doll's face.

A quick shave and a quick shower, and at 9:01 AM I am at the local op-shop dropping off Charlotte.

Since then, I heard no more voices in the house. I wondered to myself if the other 999 dolls Ms. Jo had given to their new owners had the same effect on them.

I, for one, am not game to find the answer, nor to find Ms. Jo again.

COMRADESHIP

Ismael Fernandez grew up in Wilcox, Idaho, a town of seven-hundred and twenty-one folks surrounded by tall hop plants and short alfalfa fields. He lived with his grandparents in a home built on land where his grandfather, a Vietnam War veteran, once picked beets and onions.

As life happens, both grandparents perished in a farming accident which led Ismael to the nearby orphanage in Roxbury, Idaho.

When Ismael arrived at the orphanage, he surveyed the large dormitory which held over 100+ beds, all lined up in two rows that seemed to go on forever. He settled into his single bed at the north end of the building and noticed the stream of young boys similar in age to him as they strolled into the dormitory. He found himself in a different world than the one he once had back in Wilcox.

The boys streamed in, in two distinct flows. One flow comprised very brown faces, and the other comprised more pale, white faces, each of them looking at each other in a distrusting manner.

Ismael was dumbfounded at the atmosphere in the room as they settled into their beds. Brown faces were to the north side of the building, while white faces were to the south side of the building.

As twilight descended, all the boys felt the sombre feeling of sleep come upon them. As did Ismael.

An hour must have passed, when Ismael heard whispering voices around him, the rustling of sheets, and many little brown faces getting out of their beds. They started moving their beds into mounds of beds frames, mattresses and pillows, into a beautiful wall.

Every few minutes, the boys stopped to listen to make sure that no one had noticed the activity, which they had not.

As they continued, a few of the boys dragged out several small wooden boxes. Once Ismael saw them open, he saw in the glimmering moonlight the shining spectre of marbles. Thousands of marbles, of all sizes and colours, laid before him in several boxes, with all the boxes placed two feet behind the overturned beds frames, mattresses and pillows.

Ismael kept quiet and let the brown-faced boys continue setting up what seemed to be a fortress behind the protective wall. Then he saw a most amazing thing.

Several boys had climbed onto each other's shoulders and were reaching above them. They opened the panel in the low hanging ceiling to reveal 20 to 30 gridiron helmets, which they brought down, and started distributing them.

Ismael received a beat-up helmet that still showed specks of old paint, mingled with mud and grass, and what even seemed like dried blood. However, he did not hesitate in following the other boys, and placed said protective helmet on himself. He noticed that all the boy's helmets had a safety guard, but he did not. But then again, he was new and not sure what was going to happen.

The boys finished, and their brown faces were quiet. Only the moderate breeze outside could be heard moving the close by tree branches.

'So now what?' thought Ismael.

In whispering voices, he heard one brown-faced boy—who appeared to be the leader—say to the boys.

'Get ready.'

The boys gathered as many of the loose marbles as they could hold in their tiny hands and stood behind the protective wall. The brown-faced leader yelled, 'War!'

Hundreds of marbles of all assorted sizes and colours flew out of the boys' hands, heading towards the dark south side of the room, and all hell broke loose.

Bouncing marbles ricocheted from the walls. Some hit their targets since Ismael heard screams and crying.

Mayhem was occurring in front of him, and it caught Ismael in the middle of it. He was not sure why it was happening, but sensing the exhilaration of the brown face boys, he too picked up a handful of marbles and hurled them toward unseen victims.

Suddenly, Ismael felt a smack on his left cheek and fell to the floor, realising a marble had hit him by the return fire. The startled white-faced boys had recovered from the surprise and initial shock and had recovered loose marbles around them and hurling them back toward the north side of the building where they had originated.

It must have been five minutes at most, but it seemed like hours had passed when the lights in the dormitory lit up, showing three of the biggest matrons Ismael had ever seen standing. They were screaming orders and getting in the middle of the fracks, stopping all activity.

Rubbing his left cheek and sensing a slight bump developing, Ismael surveyed the outcome of the night's effort and was in awe.

The walls were all dented, with small indentations where their missiles had landed. Broken windowpanes were on both sides of the room and glass was all over the floor, ensuring that those unfortunate enough to step on them got a couple of good cuts.

The matrons achieved order, forcing all the boys (brown-faced and white-faced alike) to stand at attention and look at each other. Both rows of boys' faces held a serious look. As the matrons turned to head to their rooms, Ismael could see smiles appearing on both sides of the aisles. The boys realised they were not enemies, but that the 'war' had created an 'incident' that the matrons would have to deal with—costly at that also—but one that had united them for once.

From that incident onward, Ismael saw a distinct atmosphere change in the orphanage as the brown-faced and white-faced boys bumped into each other in the hallway. They did not fight, but they had found comradeship.

CUT FLOWERS

You are to me like the amaryllis because you are worthy beyond beauty.

My life with you is like the anthurium because of the happiness you bring to me.

The aster represents the patience you show for all my crazy things.

While the chrysanthemum epitomises the fidelity of your love for me.

Thank you for bringing all of this into my life.

In a vase of cut flowers.

CONCORD RHETORIC ASSOCIATION OF POETS

D isgusted. Shameful. Vulgar. Rude. Uncouth.'

Those are some of the printable words used to describe me. You would think that the President of the Concord Rhetoric Association of Poets would have a better vocabulary to draw on as part of her repertoire of adjectives.

Why all this convolution, you might ask yourself?

All they had asked me to do was to generate a massive banner for our annual association booth. Our booth was to be inside the large auditorium of the Concord Civic Centre for the Hume Council Writers Festival.

My assignment: to ensure that the expense of said banner was on budget, and that a local business could make the banner, thus supporting the local economy of the council. I did that.

Hume Printers were owned and run by the same home-grown family, now going on sixty-four years. So, how much more local and supportive could I have selected?

Not only did Hume Printers develop the banner to specification, but under–I repeat–under, budget.

So, what was the problem? I said to the President of the Concord Rhetoric Association of Poets, as we stood under the enormous banner in the auditorium.

She then pointed up to the banner: Hume Council Writers Festival Presents: C.R.A.P.

The President of the Concord Rhetoric Association of Poets glanced at me with contempt and then stormed out of the room.

What did I do?

THANK YOU GUMAN

The naked eye easily saw the seven lights. The crowd gathering in the reception area of the Parkes Observatory in New South Wales (NSW) was tense, waiting for the principal speaker to come to the podium and address them.

'All I can say is that we are dumbfounded as to this matter,' stated Dr. Frederick Gilmore of the Parkes Observatory. He was standing in the observatory reception area, where a group of about twenty journalists and various organisation personnel had gathered to examine and ask questions about the phenomenon that took place over the skies of Northport, NSW.

'My colleagues, Dr. Emilia Simpson, at the Paul Wild Observatory and Dr. Michael Smith, of the Siding Spring Observatory agree with me.' He spoke, 'Our telescopes do not penetrate the dark haze enough to allow us to see the lights in more detail.'

'Dr. Gilmore, this is Peter Lawrence from the Sydney Gazette. What about other world observatories? Are they able to see more than us?'

'We have been in contact with the Gran Telescopio Canarias in the Canary Islands, the world's largest, as well as Mauna Kea Observatory in Hawaii, the US—where Keck 1 and Keck 2 are located—and also with the Paranal Observatory in Chile. They are all also stumped by this event.'

'Dr. Gilmore, how is it possible that we can see the lights by the naked eye, and yet our telescopes cannot see any more than our eyes?' asked Peter Crayford of the Daily Bugle.

Paul Fontanilla, from the Archaeological Biblical Research Foundation, interrupted the conversation with his question, 'Dr. Gilmore, do you believe the sounds emitted from the stars is the voice of a supreme being trying to communicate with us?'

Another interviewer shouted, 'Dr. Gilmore, could these be alien starships trying to communicate to us in some unknown language, or variation of a language we do not understand?'

'Dr. Gilmore,' shouted Abigail Kent, from the Brisbane Astronomical Society, 'Please give us something we can share with our readers, anything!'

The journalists kept asking Dr. Gilmore a barrage of questions. In a far corner, holding a mop, was a 69-year-old janitor by the name of Alfie Tindall, an Aboriginal elder of the Gundungurra tribe. He was a rather short, stocky-built individual who, while tattered with the furies of time, had a mind as sharp as any young person. As he heard more questions being asked to Dr.

Gilmore, Alfie remembered his grandfather Guman telling him a story when he was young, incredibly young.

'Alfie, long ago, when there was nothing. The seven birrung (stars) appeared, and the bamal (earth), badu (water), burra (sky), guwing (sun), yanada (moon) and the warriwul (Milky Way) appeared, where there was once nothing, and all was good.' He went on, 'Then the dimaru (tree) appeared, then the garuma (black bream) swam in the badu (water). Then you would see the ngurra (bird's nests) and all the different binyang (birds) could be seen flocking together in the burra, as if in harmony with nature.'

Alfie would listen, and Guman would continue his storytelling. 'Then, Alfie, as the bamal was forming the world, it saw the first burumin (possum) and wumbat (wombat). Then the seven birrung would appear even brighter in the burra, and great sounds of murungal (thunder) would fill the sky, and flashes of huge mungi (lighting) would light up the sky, making everything on the earth, sea and sky stop in awe.'

As a young child, Alfie would hear his grandfather tell these stories, and he was fascinated by the colourful story his grandfather had woven for him, to either entertain him or to put him to sleep late in the evening. But one thing he remembered for sure was the last two parts of the story.

'My young grandson,' said his Guman, 'The first dyin (woman), saw the seven stars and heard the seven lights speak to her in a voice she understood. She knew not how, but it was melodic, smooth. Then she gave thanks to the seven stars for all they had given her and they were happy for her.' His Guman went on, 'As the first dyin saw more and more of her land, sky, her water and her animals, she thought she would like to have someone to share all those beautiful things. The dyin spoke to the seven stars and asked for a gamarada (comrade). The seven stars spoke back to her, telling her that instead, she would have a mula (man). She knew she would share all her things with him. Together they became dyinmang (wife), and mulamang (husband). They would have many duruninang (daughters) and many durung (sons), and the land would fill up for many years with their descendants.'

His grandfather would continue his story solemnly, which took Alfie by surprise, but he knew, even at such a youthful age, that something terrible had happened. 'Alfie, as the dyin became a dyinuragang (old woman) she also became a mubi (mourner at a funeral), but not for her husband but for the seven stars, for they had disappeared and she knew what that meant. Alfie, my young damali (namesake), it meant that the world would end when the stars reappeared and if the offspring could not speak to them.'

Alfie sensed a calm in the crowd and saw people dispersing solemnly, looking like no satisfactory answers were given, despite how many questions they had asked. He then approached Dr. Gilmore and asked, 'Dr. Gilmore, have you sent a message to the seven stars in any way?'

The question slightly took Dr. Gilmore by surprise, but Alfie had asked a valid question. He replied, 'Yes, we have transmitted to the stars a welcoming message in all the 195 languages in the world. But no, we have received no reply.'

'How are you sending these messages?' he asked.

Looking haggard but patient, Dr. Gilmore answered Alfie, 'We have a radio wave telescope here at Parkes that you speak into it, and it translates our words into radio waves. These are then received by the seven stars in a matter of seconds. We keep it on twenty-four hours a day, awaiting a response - any response, no matter how small. If no one is there when a message is received, it is recorded, translated and printed out through the printer.'

'Oh, OK. I see,' said Alfie, gathering his mop and continuing with his daily chores. The observatory would close soon. Dr. Gilmore smiled as he saw the old man walk away, and he thought to himself, 'Well, he at least asked better questions than all those damn reporters!'

He walked towards his office to finish the day.

As the staff of the observatory filed out of the building, and the light dimmed in all the offices and communal areas, the short and stocky man moved unseen into the shadows. He headed towards the telescope department and opened the doors. Not seeing anyone there, he went through and closed the door behind him.

He approached the telescope and picked up the microphone. He took a big deep breath, relaxed, and started speaking in the language of the first dyin, remembering everything his grandfather had told him and everything his mother had also taught him as a young man. He spoke for what seemed a lifetime. He spoke eloquently, describing the world humans all lived in, how humans tried to preserve it—sometimes not too well, but mostly—and how much humans care. Alfie stressed how much humans cared. He was not sure why; it just was something he felt and wanted the seven stars to know. He hoped that was what the seven stars wanted to hear. It was just his heart speaking.

After twenty minutes, Alfie laid the microphone down and stood by, waiting for a response. He wasn't sure how long it would take to get an answer.

Alfie got up, thinking he had failed in trying to help the rest of humanity, until the speakers of the radio wave telescope emitted a message in an unfamiliar language.

Alfie heard it but could not understand it. What did it all mean?

The printers came to life, printing the strange spoken words out. Alfie looked at the printout and read the message:

'Our children. We are happy to hear from you. We are happy for you. We just wanted to know if you were all right. The words spoken by the first woman were received and understood. We are responding to you in another ancient language. We hope you know you will always be part of us. Until forever. Mother.'

Alfie smiled and wondered what Dr. Gilmore would think of this.

He discreetly left the telescope department. As he exited the Parkes Observatory, he looked up into the night sky and noticed that the seven stars were no longer there. His mission was complete. He got into his car and headed home. He gave thanks to his guman for the story told long ago.

His story might have just saved the Earth.

I REMEMBER

We met at the Westin around 5; I was on time, but you were not.

You might not remember it.

We walked down the quay and we dined alone.

There was music for us to hear.

You might not remember it.

Those dazzling January moons. It warms my heart to know you might remember it the way I do.

How often I think of that night.

You wore a dress of blue, or was it white?

You might not remember it.

How young you were, how strong I was. I felt like a prince in your arms.

Now as the clouds in our minds gather more strongly and memories fade, I say to you:

I remember.

INHERITANCE LUCK

The letter I receive from my late uncle's solicitor can only be, well, crazy. The letter states that my late uncle has left a formidable sum of money in his will to me, with the condition that I marry the first maiden I see on the street. I race down to the solicitor's office in the Northport CBD to verify the validity of this letter.

Having confirmed the validity of the letter, I sit outside his office and wait until dusk, pondering my dilemma—not who I might bump into on the street—but my dilemma of which road to go on.

If I choose Bond Street, all the individuals on the street will be bankers. I cannot imagine what life will be like married to someone with banker hours. That will not do.

If I choose Broadway Street, in the arty-farty area of town for sure, the theatre type would befall me. Goodness, an actor in the family. That will also not do.

A choice of Harlequin Street is also out of the question. The street is full of bookstores, flower shops and newsagents. Imagine someone in the family with those hours? That will not do for sure.

Selecting Downing Street will for sure encapsulate all possibilities in the arena of politics, and no one would ever want that in their lives. You know the type, politicians that will shake your hand before an election, and your confidence after that. That is out of the question.

So, I decided that the safest street is Bright Street—so named in the last century for the gas-lit lamps that adorn both sides of its pristine cobblestone pavement, that still in this modern age must be lit each early evening by hand. There, I would find an attractive maiden for me to approach for matrimony.

As dusk descended and as luck would have it—in what I can only call as 'inheritance luck'—I arrive at Bright Street unseen by anyone. As I walk down the gauntlet of lit gaslights, a robust wind blows, and all the lights go out.

Blackness envelopes me.

As I continue to walk, I see no one. I cannot see my hand in front of me. It is so pitch black with all the gaslights off.

My travel is now a slow process. I do not want to trip and hurt myself. Nor do I want to bump into anything that might have a sharp edge and cut myself.

The two things I hope for in my trek to accomplish my task, as prescribed by my late uncle's will, are that an attractive maiden shows up as soon as possible; and second, that I do not walk into Cemetery Road and find someone there.

MY LIFE AS A TWIN

I am often asked what my life as a twin is like. Being a twin has its benefits, but it also comes with an exclusive set of rules. Whether you did everything together, or you were an independent twin growing up, there are rules that will set you apart.

Let me describe some rules.

Under no circumstances are you to go on a date with a woman that your brother set up for himself, and now wants to get out of.

Never do a switch between your wives. They know.

Of course, simple little rules can be bended a bit. You can, for example, show off your baby and toddler pictures and tell people you are the handsome one.

Your friends assure you they can look at the photos and they can tell who is who. I can tell you — not going to happen.

Growing up, twins are always being tested. Your friends test you and your brother to see if you have telepathic powers. We do not, but if my brother and I ever said the same thing simultaneously, well, everyone's mind would get blown away. This also happens to non-twins, and it's no big deal, but when twins do it–wow, then it's spooky.

For the record, when I am asked if we played tricks on my teachers, friends and parents, the answer is yes. But when we are again asked to tell a story about what trick we pulled, we will not answer, because the tricks were dumb, boring, and lame.

On the positive side, being a twin has a few perks.

A day spent shopping with your brother is incredible, because your brother can try on clothes for you when you're too lazy or cannot go to the store, and you know they will fit you when he brings them home.

Have you got two job interviews on the same day at 10 AM? No problem. You can go to one, and your brother can go to the other. Simple.

At parties, I am often asked how it feels to be a twin, frequently with my brother standing next to me. I have answered with: 'I do not know. He is adopted' — the look on the face of the person is priceless.

But the best part of being a twin is that you cannot imagine what your life would be like without your brother as your partner in crime.

MY FAVOURITE BIRD

I cannot say that there is friction between my mother-in-law and me. There are, however, moments when the old battle-axe can make me lose my temper with her coaxing and cajoling and her sarcastic remarks about my physique, my job, and overall disposition.

However, put up with it I do, because at the first sign of resistance, WWIII starts, and it upsets my wife and the kids. So, I grin and bear it. Until the day that sweet revenge came to my help.

It is a typical lunch get together on the weekend, and the old woman is at one of her best moments of incessant tormenting. My wife says that she needs to run out to the grocery store and grab a couple of things missing for lunch.

So, into the SUV she goes, with the kids in tow, and the old battle-axe stays with me. There is no way my wife ran out of stuff; I think to myself. All she wanted was peace for a moment, and so she left me in my torture.

About ten minutes after my wife's departure, I hear tap-tap-tap-tap-tap-tap in the house and wonder what in the world it is.

The old witch also heard the tap-tap-tap-tap-tap-tap. Every minute, the tapping keeps repeating itself.

Tap-tap-tap-tap-tap-tap.

Tap-tap-tap-tap-tap-tap.

Tap-tap-tap-tap-tap-tap.

The old hag asked, 'Do you hear that infernal tap-tap-tap-tap-tap-tap'? Is someone at the front door?'

Opening the front door and stepping out to look, I saw no one. I said no and left it at that.

The tapping continues and the old woman is now going berserk, going from room to room, and searching for the demonic 'tap-tap-tap-tap-tap-tap' She searched the entire ground floor.

The taps continue.

Then she wobbled down to the basement. But again, no luck.

The taps continue.

She does a Sir Edmund Hillary and up to the bedrooms she went. She called out to me to join her saying, 'Enough of you not doing anything! Get up here and help me find this excruciating tap'.

So, I did.

As she continues looking room to room, the tapping continues. I could hear her mumbling to herself, cursing and opening doors, and closing them to no avail. Glancing out the master bedroom window, I see the cause of the drumming producing that reverberatory sound — tap-tap-tap-tap-tap-tap—that can be heard at some distance.

I think to myself, that woodpecker is my favourite bird in the world.

I stay quiet and smile.

Competing TV reporters were scurrying left and right at the scene, each trying to set themselves and their camera crew up at the best angle to present the news to their audience.

The police were also busily running their crime scene tape to cordon off the area, attempting to preserve what evidence they could from contamination by the reporters (or from any of the onlookers that usually arrived when there was a disaster or crime).

From where I stood, I could see the entire scene—the onlookers, the reporters, the police squad cars, and the detectives. Some detectives stood with note pads, writing their notes from their interviews, while others casually talked to other officers—each knowing that there was not much one could do in a situation like this. I approached the splattered remains of the body. Male for what I could see. I deduced this since he was nude and only wearing one pink glove. Yep, that was why I made detective, all right!

A body had flown out the window of the 12th-floor apartment building. Only three things could cause that to happen: suicide, accident or murder.

So, before the investigation started, I check the time: 11:30 PM. It was going to be a late one for sure.

Proceeding to the lift, I found the door of apartment 1204 open, with a uniformed officer at the entrance to keep out any unwanted intruders. I flashed my detective badge. The uniformed officer just nodded and let me in without hesitation.

The crime scene investigators were combing the area.

I saw the common apartment lounge area, well presented, well organised, and clean as a whistle. Not a thing was out-of-place other than the tilted picture frame of a single sailing boat on a calm sea, showing the door to the wall safe was open.

After one of the crime scene investigators finished dusting the safe for prints, I approached the safe door. Using my pen, I opened it more and glanced at the contents inside the safe.

After poking around with my pen, I noticed ten stacks of $100 bills neatly bundled into what appeared to be 100 bills per stack. It was enough cash to buy that Audi Q5 2.0 Sport that I had been looking at online, with a few dollars to spare to take the wife out to a nice dinner. It was all neatly wrapped.

The safe also contained a small, closed jewellery box, a small plastic transparent case containing about a hundred and twenty Krugerrands (with an approximate value of $156,000 dollars by today's prices, by my guess). An assortment of paperwork was also stacked neatly, untouched it seemed, with one lonely pink glove.

OK, so we had a nice sizeable booty for any professional, semi-professional, or amateur burglar to leave with, but nothing seemed disturbed.

A quick review of the remaining rooms in the apartment reflected the same conditions. The sliding balcony door was open in the lounge, while the master bedroom and the other two bedrooms were spotless, the kitchen was immaculate, and the bathrooms sparkled as if no one lived there. Either this guy had a germ phobia, or one hell of a house cleaning service was coming daily.

As lead detective, I gathered the troops and got the scoop on the owner of the abode.

'A Michael Pennyworth, boss,' said Detective Charlie Pride, a six-year veteran of the homicide squad, 'Works for one of the wealth funds in the CBD. Well-liked by the other tenants. Came in around 9 PM, according to the doorman, and no one came in afterward until midnight when the doorman locked the front door to all visitors, except for the tenants who all have an electronic key.'

'But he said no one came in until the police arrived,' said Officer Jamie Tennant, who had been first to arrive at 10:30 PM.

'OK, Charlie. You and Detectives Scanlon, Rodrigues, Estevez and Huang get the reports in. Then wait for the crime scene folks to run through all their data and report to me tomorrow. Also, all of you continue to interview the building tenants—yes, all sixty-four tenants, and anyone staying with them—tonight.'

'I want it all done by morning,' I said, as I walked out the door, pointing to Detective Sally Flint to come out with me to the hallway.

'Flint, I need you to inventory all the stuff in the safe tonight. Then I need you get as much information on the company, the directors, co-workers, and anyone in Pennyworth's personal life—family, friends, lovers—and anything you deem appropriate in our investigation. We will meet at my office at 5 PM and go over all the facts we have with the rest of the team. The forensics team should be complete by then.'

'Sure, Boss,' said Flint.

Glancing at my watch, I saw the time. Great, 3AM. I would surely wake up Bella when I came in. But then she was used to it, and the kids were all out of the house, so maybe I won't, I thought to myself.

As I drove home to catch a few winks, I kept thinking of the nude body of Pennyworth with one pink glove and the second pink glove in the safe. What did it mean?

At 5PM, the squad gathered in the conference room and hashed out all the specifics of the case.

First and most important, no prints were in the apartment other than Pennyworth's, so either he had no visitors or, if he did, they had wiped the prints off.

Second, it appeared nothing was taken, so burglary was off the table.

Third, there was no suicide note. Besides, why would Pennyworth open the safe, take off all his clothes, put on one pink glove, leave the other in the safe, leave the safe door open, open the balcony sliding door, and step off into the beyond?

Fourth, CCTV cameras showed Pennyworth arrived at 9:01 PM (just as the door attendant stated) and no one else came in until Officer Tennant responded to the call at 10:30PM, followed by the rest of the police force investigating the incident, including me, at 11:34 PM.

Fifth, Pennyworth had no unusual activity in his credit cards or bank accounts the weeks before his demise. His work also continued to be ordinary and not unusual in either the contents of his work or his work meetings, as per the conversions Flint had with his boss and co-workers.

Sixth, Pennyworth, while being efficient in his job, had no will written. But then again, per Flint, he also had no living relatives, so there were no suspects there to pursue either.

This case would require some in-depth research into all possibilities other than the obvious—this was the consensus of the squad team. So, I gave further delegations to the follow up to the team for them to proceed with and try to resolve.

Time passed, and a few months in, new incidents came into the squad team's portfolio to resolve. Leads on Pennyworth had turned up nothing and were as cold as the nose of an Eskimo. Unless some miraculous intervention appeared, this would become a cold case—an unsolved case.

When twelve months had passed, the chief called me into his office to go over the status of the case.

I had nothing to report.

We had no results in the last twelve months. Over 15,000 hours of work had left us in the same place as where we had started: nowhere.

So, the chief said to me that enough time, resources and money had been spent on this case and that it was time to close it, box it up, and send all the files to the cold case storage facility. That was where the last moments of Mr Michael Pennyworth's life would stay recorded, held, and unsolved.

MY FAVOURITE HOLIDAY PLACE

Ever since I was a young child, I have been an enthusiastic fan of Christmas. To me, Christmas is a place and a time where people come together, despite their differences and who they are.

People seem to be gladder and happier.

Even the thought of venturing into the maddening shopping malls does not give me anguish or make me sick with disgust, that all the stores are doing their best to sell, sell and sell. Instead, I see a multitude of people filled with joy as they go about spending time with friends, family and loved ones.

Christmas seems to bring out the best in people.

Many strangers at other times of the year would not even look at another, but during this season holiday greetings seem to fly out of their mouths so easily.

My favourite holiday place during the Christmas period has to be my home.

Growing up, I always loved seeing my parents hanging the decorations around the house, happily arguing on how to baste, cutting the turkey and, after the main meal, driving around the neighbourhood to see how the neighbours did up their homes.

Christmas is the best holiday, because just for a little while everyone believes in the impossible.

No conflicts, no wars, no hunger, no illness. That is what we wish for, hoping that on this one occasion we might be lucky enough to get our wish.

I hope people can take some of that Christmas spirit and make it year-round feeling. Christmas is a time for bringing people together and being home, and that is why it is my absolute favourite holiday place.

Gosh, I am naïve.

MY NEIGHBOURS

I have a lot of neighbours. Some I know better than others.

There is a small bell over the front door of my store which alerts me when a visitor comes in.

This little bell is not a high-tech security system by today's standards, but it is efficient enough to alert me when she walks in.

She is worthy of my look.

A lot of distinct types stroll in every week. Some are large, some are small. I find aggressive ones and sometimes timid ones, but this time she is a thing of beauty—something tells me that this is the one!

There is a look to her that stops me in my tracks; hair with a sense of multi colours—white, orange, and black—that melts me when I see her, and I know I want to close in on her and be so close as to feel her.

I can sense a fiery, a strong-will, and altogether more temperamental personality than most. This attracts me to her.

Would you call it attitude?

Was I becoming a deprave? Irresponsible. Was I totally out of control?

Oh, call me what you will, many would.

I cannot not help myself.

It is seldom that one is fortunate to have a neighbour that owns a pet grooming store next to yours where some human walks into your store with one of those beautiful Calicos.

My job catching rodents can be so lonely at night (not that is not fun, mind you), so when I watch this human bring her in, it makes my day just purrfect!

IT IS EMPTY

They do not appreciate us.

Never.

No matter what season of the year–Winter, Spring, Summer, or Fall–they do not appreciate us.

Working as an agent for the Transportation Security Administration (TSA) at a major airport in the US can be such a downer.

First, people think you are going on a power trip when you say, 'Take your shoes off.' Come on now, would you get off on something like this phrase? Of course not.

Then there is when you get to pass the 'magic wand' over a person's body as if to say, 'Look, what I found. I got you!'

Of course not.

But what must be the most amazing and spectacular thrill that we TSA agents get, is when we are going to search an individual's carry-on baggage.

Many weird things come with our job description.

We try not to smile, because if we did, we would laugh all the time.

Like the time I randomly inspected the carry-on baggage of an elegant older lady.

As I inspected the bag, I sorted its contents.

A little black book.

A small mirror.

An assortment of handkerchiefs that reminded me of the old days when a gentleman would have a handkerchief ready for a lady to use at a moment's notice (as we all know, those days are long gone).

As I sort through a few other smaller articles, I notice a little jewellery box.

When I open it, it is empty!

The lady immediately says, 'Oh, please do not let the contents spill out.'

I look at her and say: 'The box. It is empty.'

She looks at it and smiles at me like a Cheshire cat.

'Yes, it is!'

I put all the contents back into her carry-on, zip the bag up and gave it back to her. She takes it, then waves at me as she takes the left corridor to her gate and smiles.

This occasion is just one of those weird moments we have while at work. So, I thought it is all because of the season, spring; that I work at the airport and that it was my lucky day to have met one lady who now sat on her plane seat saying to herself:

'It is empty.'

MY NEXT ADVENTURE

Being garrotted to death with wires was not my idea of how I wanted to have my life ended. So, I ran like hell. You may wonder how I came to be in this predicament. Easy–It was not my fault. It seldom was.

By profession I worked at a large downtown bank in the operations centre, you know, the backbone of the organisation. I ensured all systems functioned as they should, customers assets were accounted for at the end of the night, and debits equaled credits—the basis of accounting.

I veered a bit from my daytime career at night since my tendencies were toward more of a stealth job (or as the men and women in blue like calling it—break and enter (B&E)).

Now I was not the violent burglar. No, I considered myself a gentleman burglar. I took care not to disturb the residence or establishment I might be illegally gaining access to, and always locked up after myself, as to not hint at my presence.

So, how did these two divert career paths convene, you ask?

One day, purely by accident mind you, I was screening some code on my banker's computer, and a query brought up the fact that a few of the bank's clients were in the–shall we say 'rich side'–of the monetary equation.

Cascading in front of my eyes, were hundreds of clients' names, addresses, source of income, and detailed descriptions of assets–many assets. I found rare coins and vintage postage stamps, antique books and paintings. All with exquisite dollars signs assigned to them and so easily in reach.

I thought to myself, how is it that these individuals all have these wondrous objects scattered throughout all the different suburbs in Sydney? Should they not be in one central location so that I could better appreciate them? For instance, somewhere close, like my ex-brother-in-law's shed? My ex-brother-in-law, Oscar, who was currently incarcerated for those minor mistakes we all make, like bringing a gun into a convenience store and showing it to the Pakistani clerk, who I am sure had seen one of those before.

In all the confusion that followed, the police apprehended him. He went to trial and was given a 15-year sentence in Goulburn Prison. He had only served three, since he did not appreciate the advances he received from several amorous individuals, and escaped. He now lives–you guessed it–in Pakistan under the convenience store clerk's name. How he is getting away with it is another story, so let me get you back to mine.

We all started young, I guess. You know, I picked up a pencil in school and it remained in my pencil case. I took a book from the school library out for a report, but then I 'forgot' to return it. A visited the doctor's office, signed the insurance paperwork, and the pen found itself in my shirt pocket. A simple bump into someone and their wallet wound up in my hand. Then it was my first B&E—my ex-father-in-law's bookstore.

It just happened.

One night, over cocktails, someone mentioned that they were looking for a first edition of Jerome McKinley's 1803 *Swann Songbook* and was not willing to pay the going retail price of $35,000 but would pay $17,000. I knew that there was one such copy in a very familiar bookstore.

So, before you could write a sonnet to your wife, I carefully entered my ex-father-in-law's bookstore, disarmed the alarm, got the book, armed the furious alarm again, and walked out. All this was extremely easy since I had a key to the store, knew the alarm code, and knew precisely where the book was. I had made sure it was in an accessible location the week before.

So, for less than 20 minutes of work, my mattress felt a little lumpier with 340 Edith Cowan's under it, after I disposed of the book.

After that experience, I realised one thing—being a burglar was fun. I liked it. Just like I loved working in the bank's operations centre.

To master my newfound talent, I knew I needed an education. So, with my new stash I slowly accumulated a cluster of deadbolt lock, electronic surveillance and alarm system manuals and other necessities for my new career.

On the pretext of embarking on a writing career, I visited many of the minimum-security penitentiaries in New South Wales. My 1998 Ford GLi Sapphire accumulated many kilometres as I travelled from Berrima Correctional Centre to Tamworth Correctional Centre (and points in-between), interviewing inmates to see what it was they did so wrong for them to accept an invitation to their respective accommodations. By the way, I found my research fascinating since I never knew how many innocent individuals there are in correctional facilities these days.

Now I was ready to graduate and go out on my own.

A Mr Franklin DeLario popped up in my list (a nice photo showing a 70-year-old distinguished-looking fellow) as the proud owner of the ring which the late John F. Kennedy had used to propose to Miss Jacqueline Bouvier. It was a beautiful 2.84-carat emerald and 2.88-carat diamond engagement ring, which set Mr Kennedy back a little over $1,000,000.00 in 1953. Designed by Van Cleef & Arpels, its unique design made the ring stand out, and the combination of baguette stones, diamond accents and emeralds with diamonds made it an exciting and memorable engagement ring.

I fell in love with it as I read the insurance appraisal and its current value of $12,000,000.00. I knew it would make it an excellent addition to any discriminating oil sheik, mainland China tuhao, or a Russian oligarch.

Subsequently, a visit to Mr Franklin DeLario was in the making. With my newfound knowledge, I found out that Mr DeLario lived in an average, but distinguished home in Randwick. It was not wealthy by some of the other home's standards in the area but had a well-manicured lawn that showed the man had a taste for the beautiful things in life.

I arrived with my pizza box in one hand (pepperoni, in case you speculated), a lovely blonde wig (Warhol-like), gloves on, and my Cronulla Sharks cap (I hate the Sharks). I proceeded up the steps from his front lawn to the front door, where immediately I noticed the homeowner had installed the Maitland Security System. It was not your very top of the line system, but it was not too shabby either.

Like in most modern alarm systems, when this system detected an intrusion, it allowed for a small time for the alarm to be disabled before it called the police. This alarm also enabled the use of direct sensor broadcasts to trigger the system.

Confusing, right? Yes, it was confusing if you did not know what you were doing. However, a simple reconfiguration of the outside wires was the Achille's heel of this system—according to William 'Shakes' Winford, current living at Tamworth facility—who explained how to disable it during one of my 'interviews.'

However, the alarm was not armed. Interesting, I thought.

Now, for the front door locks.

The homeowner had installed the HDC-HRC Captive Key Hercules Deadbolt lock, assuming this and its electronic alarm would deter a burglar. They surely would, but I was better than your average neighbourhood burglar, and a few twists with my easily concealed lock picks made it easy prey for me. Again, interesting enough, the front door was unlocked.

Fascinating.

Before these actions, I had made sure no one was home. I rang the home number twice in two 10-minute intervals, with no answer. I rang the doorbell again, twice, and again no one came to the door. Even though there was one solitary light in the front bedroom upstairs, I knew no one was home—or at least, so I thought.

I reached the rear master bedroom and found—as many folks do after they believe they have their fortress secured—a small jewellery box in the Missus' dresser, laid ready for my picking.

Opening it, I saw the splendorous ring. Even by the moonlight coming in through the bedroom window, it radiated beautifully.

As I lifted the ring from the said box, and place it in my left front pant pocket, a shadow appeared from behind me, and I felt a metal wire come around my neck.

Surprised, I raised my hand, pushed the wire up, ran, and immediately stumbled on the body of Mr DeLario laying face up, white as a mackerel and out cold. Someone was standing over me with menacing eyes.

Having not bargained for this, I kicked my right foot up and—as if by guidance—struck the groin of the shadow who let out a big 'oof'. He fell on his knees, not expecting my reaction. I pushed him, and he hit his head on the corner of the bedpost — knocked out cold.

I gathered my thoughts as shadow man lay there—a hefty sort but not muscular. He was medium built and not quality burglar material or a potential murderer by my book.

Quickly I went down the stairs, realising that someone had committed a murder. Realising I had forgotten to check Mr DeLario's vitals, I went back upstairs and made sure he was OK. I placed the ring in the shadow man's pocket.

The difference between a gentleman burglar (*Moi*) and a cat burglar, is that a burglar worries when the owner or resident of the home will return while a cat burglar goes in when the owner or resident is in residence — they do not worry about an interruption.

Shadow man was a cat burglar who committed a crime. I was a gentleman burglar and a good citizen. Upon my departure I made an anonymous call to 000 from one of those rare things these days — a payphone — and reported a suspicious person or persons, at Mr DeLario's home.

The next morning the Sydney Gazette printed a short story on page six. The short story detailed the capture of a cat burglar by one Mr Franklin DeLario, who received several injuries while battling said cat burglar — a brave man. No articles were reported stolen from the home by the New South Wales police.

After reading the story while having my morning breakfast at home, I felt delightful, and I headed to work. Sitting in front of my computer, I reviewed the bank's client files and sat there pondering what would be my next adventure.

THE HUNTER

It is gratifying to know that I am the best at what I do. I know I am.

In 2006, at the tender age of sixteen, Doctors Chittenango Pandrade and BS Stamatis of the National Institute of Mental Health and Neurosciences in Bengaluru (Bangalore), India, knew it. They met with me when I visited India with my parents. While in my meeting with these marvellous doctors, I discovered I am a hunter.

My prey is small, so it is difficult to pick and find. However, my perseverance enables me to reach that pinnacle of every hunter in the world—the capture of said prey.

The doctors reasoned that there are some common habitual behaviours that all hunters have—no matter what their socioeconomic background is. So, hunters from a lower socioeconomic status and hunters from a middle-class family or higher-earning household all shared in this prowess.

The readers here also have this trait, even though you will deny it, hide it, or even dismiss this tendency as a denial of nature. I will say it here. We are all hunters.

Some hunters get their prey and eat it instantly. Other hunters play with their prey for a while, as if the moment of capture will remain forever in their mind.

Others, once the prey is within their grasp, look at it and wonder how intelligent the hunter was in catching this prey, for yes, my reader, this prey is clever.

I always strive for the most common of captures. The catch and release method. This is always the best method, no matter the size of the catch.

I do this quickly because my mother is always saying: 'Peter, stop picking your nose, it is disgusting.'

STRANGE THINGS ARE HAPPENNING IN THE OKEFENOKEE SWAMP

Many folks might believe in ghosts, spirits, phantoms, shades or apparitions. Many people did, but I for one did not.

As a young child visiting my grandmother down Waycross way, about 385 kilometres south of Atlanta, I took a wrong turn. Sometime into the premature demise of the evening, I zigged where I should have zagged (no global positioning satellites in my young days) and found myself on an old dirt road. I got out of the car and stood there in a forbidden land — the Okefenokee Swamp.

Mind you now, this was not my first visit to my grandmother. Frequently I was asleep in the back seat as my dad drove his 1949 Ford Custom Club coupe (which had a suspension system that, if you could cook inside the car, you would have scrambled eggs without beating them). This time, however, I was on my way to my first year at the Coastal Open Environmental and Technical College (COETC).

I was not much of a book-smart-type-of-guy and I had learned that COETC offered service learning.

What was service learning, you ask?

Well, service learning as a teaching and learning method that used a combination of academic course content and relevant service with community agencies. You got to do a lot of stuff outside of the classroom and still finish college. It was sort of a university degree for dummies, but I am not sticking to my original story here so let me get back to it.

Derived from its Seminole name, the 'Land of Trembling Earth' was a mixture of beauty and terror. On the beauty side, the Okefenokee had exotic flowers, among them an abundance of floating hearts, lilies and rare orchids. Giant tupelo and bald cypress trees, many festooned with Spanish moss, provided a beauty that hid the likes of wild black bears, bobcats, huge alligators and tales of ghosts, spirits, phantoms, shades and apparitions.

Many folks said that odd insects existed only in the Okefenokee. I recalled, old man Leroy Barnacles-Smith told me the story, and I quote here word for word, 'See that honey a-sitting' up there on the shelf? Well, I crossed my bees with lightnin' bugs, so they could see how t' work at night, an' they make me now a double crop o' honey every year.'

The Okefenokee Swamp was a refuge for native American Indian people, escaped slaves, deserters during the Civil War, and others who were seeking concealment. Many people died and their bodies were never found.

But the one story I heard from my grandmother was the story of Atticus 'Bubba' Humphries, the headless man.

Atticus 'Bubba' Humphries went fishing along the tracks at Parsons Creek, at the beginning of the Okefenokee near Waycross. He fell asleep one night with the rails as his pillow. A train appeared, sounding its whistle frantically, but there was no response. Steel wheels kept on rolling and poor old Atticus, well, misplaced his head after that encounter.

The legend is that you could see the body walking the rails at night, swinging a phantom lantern in search of its head. My grandmother claimed my grandfather went in search of the 'shade' one night. Sure enough, it approached, solid white and six feet tall, walking directly toward Gramps, who fired a futile shot before fleeing.

The tale left me in fear for my life, and I could hear my grandmother saying to herself, 'Where has that boy gone to? Sure, as heaven is above, he is in mischief.'

I would have to agree with grandmother because as I stood there in the lonely road, with nothing but pine trees on either side and the thickest fog you have ever seen, wondering which way I should go, I saw Atticus 'Bubba' Humphries coming at me.

I jumped into my car, but it would not start—as if all the energy of the battery had evaporated and became a part of the fog.

There he stood, pointing his long index finger at me, and waving it left and right as if to say which way do I go to find my head?

He continued to do this until I rolled my window down and pointed to my left. His arm came down, and he walked into the swamp, disappearing with the mist.

A few minutes passed, and I sat there amazed at what had happened. I reflected on my previously made statements that there were no ghosts, spirits, phantoms, shades and apparitions. Yet, I saw what I saw. If I were to tell this story, I would be considered another of those Georgia country bumkins everyone tells their daughter not to mess with–and for sure not to contemplate marriage at all with the likes of me.

But I saw what I saw. There are some strange things happening in the Okefenokee Swamp.

THE FOUR DICKS

Anname Georgia is located south of its capital Atlanta by about seventy kilometres and has a population of 6,429 folks, scattered around the centre of town. The population comprises ten communities of various socioeconomic levels.

Let me introduce myself. My name is Darius Owens, owner of the *Slippery Rock Bar and Grill*, open Tuesday through Saturday from 11AM until the last patron goes home.

Sitting with me this Monday evening for our weekly poker night, is Isabel Gonzalez Gutierrez de Maduro, owner of *Hair Necessities*, the only ladies' hairstyling parlour in town. Charlie Prudhomme, owner of *Charlie's Flower Shop* and retired and former sheriff of Anname, Kingston Wilford, also sits with us.

As the only African American bar owner in Anname, I have seen a lot of change in the many years I have lived in Anname. A steady flow of diversity has come into our town, emigrating from other parts of the world (for example Isabel is a single mom from Mariel Cuba and Charlie is from up the road in Atlanta, having moved here with his partner, Robert, a criminal lawyer in a big firm in Atlanta). Sheriff Kingston Roberts (we call him King, by the way) hails from Yankee land—New York.

We know this consortium of characters as Anname's own Sherlocks, since we have helped the local constabulary solve one of two minor incidents in our town.

Notoriously referred to by the current sheriff Walton Cosgrave III as the local 'dicks', we seemed to have made him our unlikely nemesis and ally combined.

We got into this 'detective work' purely by accident.

A few months ago, Charlie was at the table when he mentioned they had assigned Robert to a case involving the millionaire recluse, Brian Hollingworth's brother Marcus, who was accused of stealing a valuable set of buttons owned by the late Button Gwinnett. That is correct, yes, the Button Gwinnett–the second signer of the Declaration of Independence representing the State of Georgia. The button collection, enclosed in a case with a transparent glass top, was on display in an exhibition at the local old town hall during June and July. I knew this because I took some time off, went down to the old town hall, and saw the buttons engraved with a big 'BG' on all seven of them.

I learned a few things about this case.

First, I had not known that Button Gwinnett was the second signer of the Declaration of Independence (who remembers who comes in second anyway). Second, I had not known that he collected buttons, and finally, that buttons were a collector's thing and that they had a value.

So, Charlie was sharing everything he knows with the poker group when of course questions come up.

Isabel: 'How much are they worth?'

King: 'Why would Marcus want to steal them?'

I quipped, 'Let's keep playing cards. Let Walton worry about it.'

As much as we made small talk during the game, the conversation continued to grow, like a crescendo during an orchestra playing. It was always steering to the same topic, the buttons. So much so, that we all put our cards down. I walked over to the bar and got us a bottle of Chivas Regal (I run a smart bar in case you were wondering) and pour us all a shot.

King: 'As Brian's brother, Marcus would inherit the buttons when Brian passes away, and as we all know Marcus, while not in the millionaire category like Brian, he is not doing too badly in the wealth management arena.'

Isabel: 'Besides, would it not be easier to steal them from the Hollingworth's mansion since he visits frequently, has a key to the place and for what purpose?'

Charlie: 'Maybe Marcus is running short of money and needs to steal them to raise a quick bundle, and he thought no one would suspect him. But along with Brian's fingerprints, the only other prints were Marcus's. So, who else could have done it?'

I interjected: 'King, if you were still sheriff, how would you go about looking into the case?'

King: 'Well, there are three major points to cover: means, motive and opportunity. Marcus check off all but one—motive—so that leads me to believe that someone else had a hand in this theft.'

Once more, I put in my two cents worth: 'A couple of points, the old town hall has no CCTV, is rarely filled with folks and it has no security guards, it would seem to me that anyone could have taken them.'

Isabel: 'But Darius, you are saying anyone could take the buttons, even us if we wanted to. But only the prints of the brother's Hollingsworth were on the case.'

Charlie: 'Good point Isabel. Maybe it was Brian who took them and wanted to blame Marcus.'

King: 'There is only one way to find out. Why don't we all pay a visit to Brian Hollingsworth and see if we can answer that for us?'

Again, I jumped in: 'Wait, this is going to piss off Walton, us meddling, and he will take offense from you, King, especially.'

King: 'Let's cross that bridge when we get to it. What time is it?'

Charlie: 'A few minutes after 7 PM, why?'

King: 'No time like the present. Let's go.'

After I closed the bar, we got into Charlie's pink Cadillac. Yes, a 1954 pink Cadillac, just like Elvis had. We consumed ten gallons of gas to go the three kilometres from the centre of town where my bar was in the little enclave of Woodland Hills, where the median mansion price went for $10,564,038 and had a population of 237. Now you know where the money was in Anname.

After ringing the doorbell, a stern face butler opened the door, enquired as to our purpose for a visit, and let us into the anteroom. He shortly returned and escorted us to the mansion's library, where the head of manse Hollingsworth sat reading the Wall Street Journal on his laptop.

Brian: 'Kingston, come in, my good man. It has been years since I last saw you and right before you shot and retire. How have you been? Please, all of you—take a chair.'

As we sit down in amazingly comfortable leather chairs around Brian Hollingworth, King answers: 'Doing well Brian. Let me introduce you to Ms. Isabel Gonzalez, Mr Charlie Prudhomme, and Mr Darius Owens. They are friends of mine, and we have a couple of questions about the stolen buttons we were wondering if you would not mind answering for us.'

Brian: 'Are you not overstepping your boundaries here? Is Sheriff Cosgrave going to wonder what your interest is in his case and, why are you interested, Kingston?'

Isabel: 'Mr Hollingsworth, I see no reason for your brother to want to steal the buttons.'

Brian: 'Ms. Gonzalez, what a lovely accent you have. Might I enquire from where your family is from, maybe South America?'

Isabel: 'A little closer. Miami, or to be exact Miami via Cuba.'

Brian: 'A beautiful country. Visited there many times in the 1950s before the Castro incident.'

Charlie: 'Mr Hollingsworth, if you would be so kind as to respond to Ms. Gonzalez question if you, please.'

Brian: 'Oh, the driver of the pink Cadillac. I saw you drive up in that monstrosity. Never liked them, even when Elvis drove it.'

I jumped in and asked: 'Mr Hollingsworth, you seem to avoid the question and steering the conversation into other areas. Why is that?'

Brian: 'Oh yes, the owner of the local watering hole, *the Slippery Rock Bar and Grill*, never visited your establishment, although I hear some reasonable country music take hold of the place on Friday nights.'

King: 'Brian, you seem to wander off the original question that Ms. Isabel presented to you. Why is that?'

Brian: 'Kingston, Kingston, my old friend. You know I do not venture out any more from my home. It has become quite a burden for me to step outside the front door and I rarely do so these days.'

King: 'And why is that Brian?'

Brian: 'If you must ask then you do not see the potential for illness and disease outside, or the chance of kidnapping for ransom, or just the off chance you might just trip and fall on the pavement.'

Charlie: 'Yes, but you could just slip in the tub as well.'

Brian: 'Young man, I do not bathe as you do, a man has a shower.'

King: 'Brian, do not get testy. We are just wondering why you continue to avoid the question.'

Brian: 'Kingston, I have welcomed you into my home and feel very threatened by you and your friends and your questions are simply intolerable. So, I ask you and your friends to depart.'

As Brian rose from his chair, Charlie noticed his housecoat revealed a beautiful men's Bamboo Cay, embroidered shirt. Suddenly, we all see the buttons, all seven of them.

Isabel: 'There look, King, the buttons, the buttons!'

Brian was quickly noticing his memory lapse and wrapped his housecoat around his waist. He demanded that we leave immediately.

Charlie: 'No, not yet. We need to ask you to open your housecoat and let us see the buttons.'

Brian: 'Leave, or I will call sheriff Cosgrove.'

King: 'Yes, Brian, call Walton. I am sure he would like to discuss with you the magical appearance of the stolen buttons from the old town hall and how they now are sewn into your shirt.' Seeing that he could not shake this moment away and knowing that he had no way out, Brian sunk into his armchair and let out a big sigh.

Brian: 'Well, you might as well call Walton and have him come over. Maybe we can clarify this situation.'

King: 'Before we do Brian, why? Why would you let the police arrest Marcus and charge him with theft when you knew he was innocent?'

Brian: 'Kingston, you remember when we were young and Marcus, you and I would play in the grounds of this very house, and my father would always pick on me for whatever reason he could think of, or even makeup?'

King: 'Yes Brian. I remember that he always gravitated towards you, but not Marcus.'

Brian: 'Marcus was his favourite. Marcus could do no wrong. As we grew and went off to college, got into the family business, and I made my millions while Marcus just wanted to become a wealth management adviser living on a salary, my father still did not see (nor wanted to see) my success. He wanted to see just Marcus' success. I hated Marcus for this all my life.'

Isabel: 'But why let Marcus go to jail for something he did not do, simply because you were angry at your father and jealous of his attention for Marcus.'

Brian: 'Because, because, why not? It was a simple thing to do and execute. I saw Marcus pick up the button case once without gloves; he was always a nincompoop, so crazy about the buttons, never realising the value of them. So, I knew only that besides me, his fingerprints were the only other ones on the case. I waited for the house staff to leave early as they do on Wednesday afternoon and I drove myself down to the old town hall. I parked a few blocks away and walked in, unseen by anyone. So, I opened the case, took the buttons, placed them in my pants pocket and drove home. No one was the wiser. The next morning, someone walked into the old town hall to look at the exhibition and noticed the case open. They alerted the police. The rest you know. Sheriff Cosgrove concluded it is a known fact that I do not leave the house due to all my paranoia and phobias, so I could not be a suspect. Besides no one saw me and why would I steal my buttons.'

When Sheriff Cosgrove arrived at the Hollingsworth house, and he saw what had transpired, he was fuming. We stepped into Charlie's pink Cadillac and drove into the evening, leaving Cosgrove to resolve the issues and ensuring that the correct brother received the correct blame for the crime.

The next day, the local newspaper carried the following front page news: 'Case solved by Sheriff Walton Cosgrove III. Buttons return to the owner.'

Sheriff Walton Cosgrove III declared citizens of the county had brought some facts to his attention and after careful follow-up by his department they dropped the charges against Marcus Hollingworth and released him from custody.

The article also stated that Mr Brian Hollingsworth was now under therapy at a Colorado facility specialising in stress disorders, phobias and other disorders.

Sheriff Cosgrove concluded that there had been no crime, and it solved the case.

Of course, there was no mention of the citizens involved in the story. I mean, who ever heard of four dicks solving a case.

THE NOTE

Walking is one of my favourite past times. Strolling on the beach is the type of walking I enjoy the most, because of the rewards I received after my walks - a proper goblet of wine.

I do most of my walks along the boardwalk of the small and picturesque fishing village of Marsaxlokk, in the south-eastern part of Malta.

I know the boardwalk for its exquisite fish restaurants. It also has many little bars, some chic and others grubby chic, but all with a tranquil view of the rocky beaches that Malta is so well known for.

My eye catches sight of a raised candy-striped shack with the moniker the *'Salty Máltese'*. It is sitting all by itself on a strip of rocky beach, and it merely calls out my name to come in and explore.

It comprises a veranda with six tables and a small bar outside. When you look inside, you can see an additional ten tables with a much larger bar.

I sit inside and grab the table by the window, giving me protection from the sun while enjoying the fresh breeze from outside and the cooling effect of the overhead fan.

I have, what I believe is the best of both worlds - the outside view and the indoor ambiance.

As the air touched by the sea in Malta carries a brininess which adds a subtle salty tang to the grapes grown here, I savour one of their many delicate flavours.

So, I order myself a glass of white wine and slowly gaze at the people walking up and down the boardwalk, going about their business.

Both young and old couples I see holding hands.

The occasional dog walker and the ever-present joggers make up the scenery, which seems to repeat itself as more people take to the boardwalk to enjoy the breezes and afternoon colours, as the sun and sky blend.

My eyes continue to glance left and right, and suddenly I see her.

She is strolling along the boardwalk wearing a blush floral print dress with large blossoms, in shades of pink, blue, and red, with a V-neckline, and ruffled straps. A bit of smocking at the sides adds a girly touch to the fitted waist, making this the most beautiful woman I have ever seen.

Her skin is a light cinnamon, with dark auburn hair hanging long over the shoulders, a heart-shaped face with luscious lips, and a smile that will make any man swoon. I know I am swooning when I see her.

As I am looking at her, she glances to her left, our eyes connect, and we both smile.

I do not know how it happens, but as if by telepathy this goddess enters the '*Salty Maltese*' and heads up to the bar, placing herself in such a way that she can see the entrance, the windows and my table.

As I sip my wine, I notice she is speaking with the bartender and nodding her head slightly in my direction. The bartender gives her the same wine I am savouring.

I ask the server to bring over some appetisers since I know, from experience, that wine, and no food do not settle well with me. As the server walks away, I make my decision.

I take out my little address book from my left coat pocket, tear off a blank page from the back of the book and jot down my note. I carefully fold it, ensuring that the creases are firmed and even, and walk over to the bar.

Approaching this beauty is difficult.

My experience with women has been average. I have not been a womaniser, and neither a hermit monk. But approaching this woman is a challenge for me.

Having gathered my courage, I approach her and sit next to her.

I introduce myself, and of course, the dumbest thing comes out of my mouth.

'You have such a lovely dress. My mother has one like it.'

What a disaster, I think. I have just earned a master's degree in dumbness.

However, she turns around and with a smile that captives just says, 'Thank you. My name is Duminka.'

We converse as if we have known each other for ages. In a few minutes, I feel that if there is someone out there to match me, she is it.

The server comes by with the appetiser plate and asks if she can put it on the bar. So, I turn to Dominika and ask if she would like to sit by the window at my table and she responds she would love that.

Gathering her glass, I escort her to the table, while the server places the appetiser on the table and we continue our conversation.

The minutes turn to hours and dinner is served.

We have our after-dinner drinks and the evening seems to pass slowly, as if Father Time has decided that time should slow down to give us, as they say, all the time in the world.

Having had plenty of drink, I excuse myself to use the facilities. I return to find Duminda standing outside on the veranda, looking at the beautiful Mediterranean sky and a blanket of stars across the evening sky that one would think were placed there just for the two of us.

I am in a trance of sorts, and I am not sure how it happened. As I arrive, Duminka holds her hand out. I reach for it. Our bodies inch closer and as I look deeply into her eyes, I give Duminka the sweetest kiss a man can give a woman on her lips.

It was only one kiss, but I knew that was it.

I give her my note.

Dominika takes it and reads it through the moonlit night, smiles and says:

'Yes.'

Eighteen years later, we are still married and still exploring the '*Salty Máltese.*'

A FINE MESS

Using the rocking chairs on my front porch, I am sharing a sweet Long Island tea with my good friend Ollie. We sit there, while making comments about the passing couples; the kids playing in the park across the street; and the various cars that go by every ten minutes doing what they do, carrying folks to their homes.

'You certainly have a nice porch, Stan,' says Ollie, sipping and smiling at the kids playing in the park.

'Thanks, Ollie. When I built the house, I wanted to make sure I had a nice, long, and ample porch so I could sit here on days like this and enjoy the neighbourhood. I am glad that it just added a little of cost to the original build.'

'Well, Stan. Whatever you paid extra was worth it,' stated Ollie.

As we rock slowly back and forth, Ollie points to the sky above the park and exclaims, 'What in the world do you think that is?'

As I look up into the cloudless sky, I see what I can only describe as a massive cube, slowly descending and heading toward the middle of the park. The children and their parents also see the object. They run as far away as they can as the giant cube continue its slow descent towards the centre of the park.

Ollie and I are in awe and watch as the giant cube softly lands. It does not even disturb a blade of glass. We are now standing on the porch so we can see better and see small dots in the sky hurriedly coming our way.

'Look,' said Ollie, 'It looks like either police or military helicopters heading our way. About six of them.'

I look up and have to agree with Ollie. The helicopters are indeed on their way towards the location of the cube. I say nervously, 'Ollie, I think we are going to have to leave as well. Not sure what is going to happen, but I am not sticking around.'

Just as I finish my statement to Ollie, we hear a sound that imitates a whirring noise from the large cube. A large aperture appears in the cube, which I can only conclude is a door or opening. Ollie and I then see a figure slowly emerging from the cube. The figure stands about two-metres tall. This is how tall I am, but what surprises us are the two large mechanical men (I call them men because that is what they look like) coming right behind the figure. They are enormous. They stand at least three to four metres high with large legs, arms, and what appear to be projectiles on their shoulders. Their faces… well they have no faces. Their 'faces' are a helmet but no eyes, nose or mouth– unlike the smaller figure standing in front of them.

As the figure sets foot on the park ground, both mechanical men take their position to the right and left of the cube. The character walks straight to Ollie and I. My instinct is to run back inside the house, close the door and barricade myself, and yet both Ollie and I do not move.

'Are you Ollie Campbell and Stan Wilson?' the figure asks in perfect English.

Stunned, we look at the figure, and I answer before Ollie can react. 'Yes, we are. Who are you?' I ask.

'I am known as Parliamentary One in my world, Nassirian. We belong to the Planetary Union and have been watching the planet Earth now for over a century. We feel you are ready to join our Union. We have selected both of you to be ambassadors of Earth in the Union. Ollie Campbell will handle Earth's representation in the Union's House while you, Stan Wilson, will represent Earth in the Union Congress,' answers Parliamentary One.

Both Ollie and I stand on the porch, again stunned. We can now see the six dots getting closer and larger. They are military helicopters, we surmise by the sound they make, and I estimate they will be here in less than five minutes.

'Look here, Parliamentary One. Those are Australian military helicopters and I am sure our government is just as surprised as us to see you land here in front of my house. You need to be cool and talk to them when they land. I am sure they have a lot of questions.' I say.

Parliamentary One does not say a word. He turns to the mechanical man standing to the left of the cube and nods. The mechanical man walks to the back of the cube out of my sight of vision, and we hear a loud 'whoosh' sound, like the wind blowing hard. Ollie and I see the helicopters now swing left and right in the sky as if they have no control. Then, as if by remote control, all the helicopters reverse their course back towards their departure point.

Parliamentary One looks at us and says, 'It is time for us to go. The Union is waiting to receive Earth's representatives and to formalise diplomatic relationships.'

'Wait,' says Ollie anxiously, 'I am not qualified to be an ambassador for the planet Earth. You have got to pick another person.'

'I agree with Ollie,' I respond. 'We are not intelligent enough to handle the responsibilities you suggest for the entire world.'

'Nonsense,' says Parliamentary One. 'We have been sending messages to Earth for the last one-hundred years and the only time we received a response was the time you both were camping in the Blue Mountains and used your short-wave radio to answer our call. Do you remember that?' asks Parliamentary One.

My mind races, and I can see Ollie's face going with the motion of trying to recollect that time. Suddenly, it clicks with me. Ollie and I were eight and nine respectively, and we had gone camping with our dads about sixty years ago. We had taken my dad's old short-wave transmitter. I remember we sat near a large boulder, propped the antenna up and sat for a few hours just listing to static. Then we heard a voice, 'Calling Earth.' Of course, thinking it was some local ranger, we answered, 'It is Ollie Campbell and Stan Wilson, sir. How are you?'

The voice said to us, 'You are the selected ones. Please wait for pickup,' after which there was nothing but the same static. We had not known what that meant and had forgotten all about it, and later that evening our dads came and collected us to return home.

'That was you?' I ask.

'Yes,' said Parliamentary One, 'That was our first contact with the planet Earth, and because you responded to our call, we selected you to be the future ambassadors for Earth. We are here to take you to the House and Congress of the Planet Union where you will represent Earth.'

We now hear police sirens approaching, and they are getting closer. The sound tells us they are approaching from various directions. Parliamentary One nods to the mechanical man on the left of the cube, and he moves to the centre of the park. We see him extend his projectiles upwards towards the sky, and suddenly we hear another massive whoosh. However, this time we see what appears to be a transparent globe surround the cube, engulfing it and my house.

The police cars get closer, roaring towards us, when suddenly their cars appear to stall. The sirens stop, bringing an eerie silence to the scene. The officers get out of their patrol cars and approach our house and the cube cautiously, but then they halt. There is a force field preventing them from going past a certain point. Parliament One nods, and the two mechanical men now return to their original positions in front of the cube's opening.

'Gentlemen, are you ready?' Parliamentary One asks.

'Give us a few minutes, Parliamentary One,' I say.

Ollie and I retreat to one corner of the porch, and we huddle. Ollie asks me the question I know I would have asked him, if he had not to beat me to the punch, 'Well, what do you think?'

I think about it and say aloud to Ollie; 'You know we have close to 200 nations in this world, and while overall we do a decent job, the world is in a mess. How do we expect one of these countries to be a representative of Earth in the Planetary Union? The United Nations sucks at resolving issues in our world as well. I do not see them sending a representative either that would do a decent job,' I say to Ollie.

'Neither you nor I am politicians. We have never held office and know nothing about how diplomacy works. We could screw things up for Earth,' adds Ollie.

'True, Ollie,' I say, 'The chances are we will screw up. But the chances are also in our favour. We have no genuine sentiment one way or another to sway us, and if we apply common sense, we might–just might–perform a diplomatic coup that even professional diplomats cannot do. So, for my part Ollie, I am in.'

Ollie thinks for a few seconds and then nods his head and says, 'Why not? What could be the worst that could happen?'

As we stand in our little huddle in the porch's corner, we hear a loud noise and see several military tanks surrounding the cube. However, it does not appear that they will penetrate the force field. An army vehicle appears and drives as close as it can to the force field. We see an officer of the army (we assume he is an officer of the army because of all the regalia we see on his chest), and he waves at us.

'Parliamentary One, is it alright if we speak with that man?' I ask.

'Of course, but you have less than twelve of your Earth minutes before we have to depart if we are to make the opening moments of the Planetary Union meeting,' he says.

As we approach the military man, we hear him say, 'I am General Marcus A. Holmes. What the hell is going on here?'

'Well, Sir. General,' says Ollie, 'This extraterrestrial being has come down and invited my friend and I to represent the entirety of humankind at their Planetary Union. We have accepted.'

'You cannot do that. You are not diplomats,' the General says.

'We agree, and that is why we accepted the position. We are going to represent to the Planetary Union what I hope is the best of humankind and let them see how much we have progressed and how much more we can achieve. Please tell the leaders of the world that when we return, we expect humanity to have achieved world peace, because this is what we will tell the representatives of all these planets. I am sure they will come and make contact later on to introduce trade between all the worlds.'

Without waiting for an answer, we both turn and walk back to Parliamentary One. 'Let's go, dude!' We say in unison.

We follow Parliamentary One into the cube, and the two mechanical men follow us. The opening closes behind us, and the cube ascends into the sky.

Ollie and I look out a window (for lack of a better description), and Ollie says to me, 'Well Stan, this is another fine mess you got us into.'

DO YOU?

October, my favourite month. A month which brings the beginning of springtime in my hometown of Happy Valley, New South Wales. The jacarandas bloom, and the entire area feels like a winter snowstorm just blew by, as the wind blows the delicate jacaranda petals onto the ground. A beautiful time of the year it is.

October also brings a full moon, and All Hallows Day (or Halloween as it more commonly known in Happy Valley) when the full moon of spring arrives and brings its own apparitions.

Happy Valley's neighbour, Samueltown, has Frederick Fisher's ghost to contend with. However, what a lot of folks in Happy Valley do not know is the impact of the October full moon. This full moon brings the reunion.

Happy Valley has one up on Samueltown's ghost: we have the Shaker Road Park House. The house is said to be haunted by 11-year-old Ray Bakestone, who drowned in a nearby dam on 5th October 1908. Legend has it that his lifeless body was carried back to the house and kept in the cellar, awaiting certification and burial. In 1939, the son of the owner, Adolphus Grant, died of appendicitis in the theatrette. Again, a boy's body lay in wait in this house. It is said that you can feel the children's presence throughout the house. There is also a rumour that in the tower stands a lonely woman waiting for the return of her son.

Today you will know the truth. Those previous statements were just a public relations campaign by the Happy Valley Chamber of Commerce to entice folks to visit Happy Valley, instead of Samueltown.

On All Hallows Eve, the annual reunion of the Masters happens.

Each year the spirits of the greatest Masters of Literature gather to read and critique the writings of the Happy Valley Writers group, prior to their annual book launch.

Herodotus, William Blake, John Bunyan, Dr. Samuel Johnson, and Francois Rabelais have done this for over twenty-five years. Yet, the citizens of Happy Valley are unaware of their action and help to the Happy Valley Writers group.

The writers group places their manuscript in the Shaker Road Park House's doorway on All Hallows Eve and retrieves it the next morning.

At midnight on that 31st of October, it all starts with the spirit of Herodotus - 'the father of history'—selecting passages from the writer's stories to ensure accuracy in the story.

Then comes Blake, described as *'became an artist at the age of ten, and a poet at twelve'*, who comes to oversee the soulful poems that are created by the group.

Now Bunyan, who describes himself as *'decent of a low and inconsiderate generation'* takes the helm, to review for correctness in the stories and poems that are to be published.

Dr. Samuel Johnson is next. Boswell describes Johnson as *'one of England's greatest conversationalists; an arbiter of common sense.'* Johnson grew up in poverty, so he reviews the stories of the writers to see if there is a potential for prosperity in the works.

Rabelais, a Frenchman, is last in the manuscript's review. John Canning has described Rabelais as, *'the greatest of the story-teller and the mightiest maker of laughter that this weary world has ever known.'* Rabelais is here to complete the works by ensuring that the serious writers author the stories and poems, but that they also include laughter for the reader.

The spirits have completed their tasks.

The Masters leave the corrected manuscript by the front door to be retrieved by the Happy Valley Writers and start the preparation for this year's book publication.

So, a lot happens on a full moon.

I intend to buy the book this year.

Do you?

A GOOD CHRISTMAS DOWN THE LINE

Planning my first job was, well, exciting.

I had tried so many careers in my youth and never seemed to hit upon the one thing that would complete me until now.

Like any Joe Blow, I had a regular job. Every morning I headed out to the local branch of one of the large banks that have offices all over Australia. My local branch was in the Happy Valley Central Business District, tucked between the local deli and the crystal shop.

Working at a bank had its advantages. People came in and spoke with me and shared with me all about their finances. Indeed, they did. They did not know me from a bar of soap, but because I worked at the bank, well, I was their father confessor with their finances. I proved this when Mr X (sorry I have some integrity and value for the privacy of my clients) came into my branch the other day.

'Mr Bart, I wonder if you could assist me with a particular acquisition I wish to purchase,' said Mr X to me.

'How can I be of help Mr X? Please call me, John.' I added.

'OK, John it is,' said Mr X. 'I am an avid collector of books, especially the ones that are about the royal family. I have come to you with a proposition, which I hope you may find interesting and beneficial to us both.'

It intrigued me. Only a few times did a bank customer come in and make such a proposition, so I was most interested in hearing more about this proposed scheme.

'Please, Mr X. Tell me how I can be of help,' I said.

'Do you much about the little local bookstore, *Missy's Book Shop*?' he asked me.

'I do not, Mr X. They transferred me to this branch from our main branch on George Street in the Sydney Central Business District just last week, and this is only my second week. Why do you ask?'

'Well John, there is a little book in that bookstore that I want to add to my collection, but the owner will not budge from the price. I wonder if you might acquire it for me?'

'Mr X, if the owner won't settle on a price with you, what makes you think the owner will settle on a price with me?'

'Oh, John, I do not expect you to buy it. I expect you to acquire it for me.'

It took me thirty seconds for the penny to drop. Mr X was not expecting me to negotiate a price but to steal the darn book for him.

'John, the book's price is $15,000, and the owner of the bookstore will not budge. If you acquire it for me, I will give you half the retail price. Are you interested?'

While math was not my forte in high school, I figured half the retail price was $7,500.00 for shoplifting a small book. The reward outweighed any risk.

'What you need me to do, Mr X?' I enquired.

'John, I need for you to go into the bookstore, get this little old book that has been sitting on the shelf for well over four decades. Then I need you to walk away with it, without its current owner getting any inkling that it has gone missing. The book is a child's biography of William I, also known as William the Conqueror and as William the Bastard. Purchased by *Missy's Book Shop* in 1979 by the owner's father, it has been there increasing in its value while waiting for someone to purchase it, or in my case buy it,' said Mr X.

'It seems a simple proposition Mr X. Since we both have a stake in this deal, rest assured I will do my part, as I know you will do yours. Agreed?' I asked.

'Most definitely,' said Mr X. We shook, and he left the bank, leaving me to ponder my course of action in obtaining his little book.

Of course, the challenge was to get the book, ensure that the bookstore owner did not notice it was missing, and walk out with it unobserved. So, I arrived at a plan of attack.

In the next four weeks I made myself recognisable by purchasing several books. I got interested in and purchased two books: *Millennium and Charisma among Pathans. A Critical Essay in Social Anthropology* by Ahmed Akbar, and *Architecture and Identity Towards a Global Eco-culture* by Chris Abel. The books cost me $339.45, and I was sure they now saw my face as a regular customer.

After the four weeks, two weeks in which I only browsed, and two weeks in which I made purchases, I received a question from the bookstore owner, 'You have no interest in biographies of any kind?' asked the bookstore owner each time she ran up the sale.

'Not yet,' I answered.

Each time I visited, I made a quick reconnaissance to ensure my 'acquisition book' was on the shelf and (thanks to modern technology) took a quick snapshot with my LG K10 mobile phone. I now had the ingredients for my 'acquisition.'

A book had methods to becoming a book and stitching was one of the most significant costs in a book. From the 'saddle stitching' (the most common and economic binding method) to 'sewn bound,' (one of its most expensive) this (among others) was what made collectors salivate for a book. Surely, you did not think it was William I's childhood.

I could create a similar book with the same type of binding, spine, matching colour for the cover and back, and the right number of pages. Now all I needed to do was to do the switch.

The cost for my substitute book was $145.55.

Sometimes lady luck was on my side, and she was shining on me today.

Mr X's request for the 'acquisition' came in the deep of winter. On the first of July, in Happy Valley, New South Wales got cold–averaging highs of 11C and lows of -2C. It was good winter coat weather.

Winter then required a good, large, bulky, oversized coat to be worn. This was to ensure that the cold and wind chill did not freeze you the moment you came out of your warm haven.

My favourite coat was my *Aspesi Faux Shearling-Lined Shell Hooded Parka*, which cost me a bundle and it was enormous.

You would never think that a bookstore would be busy in the middle of winter (I never would) but there I was on a Monday (I took a day off from work) and the place was hopping.

People, young and old, super-rich, rich, and not so rich, were all there. They were all looking at books, walking over to the sales counter, and making the registers sing that wonderful 'cha-ching' sound that was loved so much at all times of the year by store owners. This madness gave me my opportunity.

Hiding the imitation book under my *Aspesi*, I walked to the shelf and picked up the original biography. Before I placed the unique children's biography of William I under my parka, I noticed the price, $15.00.

Strange.

I kept the imitation book tucked into my parka and proceeded to the sales counter. I handed the owner a crisp $20 bill. She just stared at me and, without looking at the sticker price, said that it was the wrong amount–the price is $15,000.00. I pointed to the price sticker. She called over a junior assistant who confirmed the price, I received my $5 change, and walked out of the store.

As soon as I arrived home, I removed the sales sticker, contacted Mr X, and agreed on a time to deliver the book and collect my 'acquisition' fee in cash.

My total cost in acquiring the book: under $500.00. Who knew both the store owner and book collector were farsighted and thought the book was $15,000.00?

Profit: $7,000.00.

Sitting at home with the pile of bills in front of me, I realised that combining my banking expertise with my new career 'skills' might make for a good Christmas down the line.

A LESS THAN PERFECT DAY

Have you ever had one of those days that nothing goes your way? A day where no matter what you do, what you write, what you read, or who you meet, it all seems to go opposite to your intention? I mean, I know that making mistakes is a part of everyday life, but a less than perfect day. Well, it really irks you.

Sometimes the stress of a less than perfect day can be excruciating, painful, and bring you a feeling that nothing you do will succeed. I have had those types of days. I am sure you have as well.

So, for all those readers that have had one of those less than perfect days, I bring you joy knowing that Australia will begin celebrating 'A Less Than Perfect Day' next October 1st, 2022. It is to ensure that we recognise all Australians on this day.

So, do not stress. Next October 1st, challenge yourself to extra activities knowing that if you fail, well, it does not matter. Juggle basketballs in the middle of Argyle Street, sing the latest song by Jimmy Barnes as you ride your bicycle on John Street, mess with the local politicians by putting up a stand and distributing leaflets stating they are all members of the Communist Party of Australia. Think of all the things you can do and do not feel bad about it.

On this less than a perfect day, it really will not matter. Will it?

A LOVE OF BOOKS

The year is 3134 and the Royal Australian Starship, James Cook, is travelling through the fifth quadrant in the Milky Way doing standard exploration and research. The James Cook crew is composed of two-hundred and five crew members and seventeen officers. They are on a six-year mission to explore and report back to Starship command with any findings that prove of importance.

Angus T. Kirkland commands the James Cook. Captain Kirkland is a seventh-generation naval man, with over twelve years of command experience. Except for a small contingent of seventeen crew members, all members have served with Captain Kirkland before.

'Captain, Sir. May I have a word?' asks Commander Wilson Trevin.

'Of course, Mr Trevin. Come into my ready room, where we can converse,' Captain Kirkland responds, 'How can I help you?'

'Sir, we have an issue with the Holodeck which needs correcting but Engineering could not spot the issue yet.'

'Commander, please be specific. What is the issue?'

'Well Sir, the Holodeck has taken upon itself to delete all warfare training programs, all health help programs, and all other programs except for one. The only program the Holodeck is running now is 'The Thorn Birds', and it is driving the crew crazy.'

'And why is that commander?' asks Captain Kirkland.

'Captain, the Chaplain believes the Holodeck Program will turn the James cook into the orgy starship of the fleet and he is not happy,' answers Commander Trevin.

Captain Kirkland thinks about this for a moment. The original book, 'The Thorn Birds' came out in 1977, written by Colleen McCullough and set primarily on Drogheda—a fictional sheep station in the Australian Outback. In 1983 the book was made into a television series for the American public. The Holodeck Program has this program and thousands of others in its database for entertainment for the crew during its long space voyage.

But why this program? Captain Kirkland thinks.

'Commander, find the system logs and see who used the Holodeck last and see what program played last. There has to be an explanation this,' says the captain.

When the commander departs the captain's ready room, Captain Kirkland continues to review the daily reports, ensuring the starship is in top shape in case of an emergency. Within an hour Commander, Trevin, returns, and reports.

'Captain, I have checked the Holodeck system logs and determined that the last program run on the Holodeck was *'The Thorn Birds'*, and Chaplain Bell used it,' explains Commander Trevin.

'Computer, locate Chaplain Bell and request he come to my ready room. Yes, Captain,' answers a disembodied voice.

In no time, Chaplain Bell comes into the ready room and asks the captain if there is a problem.

'You know damn well there is a problem, Bell. The Holodeck is stuck on the last program it ran. It has deleted all other programs, and the last person to use the Holodeck was you. Care to explain what happened?' queries Captain Kirkland.

Sheepishly Chaplain Bell explains; 'Captain, Sir, I apologise for what has happened. I did not mean for it to happen. It just did. I became obsessed with the character Meggie Cleary, to the point that I reprogramed the Holodeck to delete the character of Father Ralph de Brassard and insert a new character—myself as Chaplain Bell. I rewrote the story from an Anglican priest's point of view, and then the Holodeck just went crazy. I did not know what to do, and I hoped engineering would find a solution before they brought it to your attention.'

'Captain,' Commander Trevin interrupts, 'Engineering has found only one solution for the current situation in the Holodeck. They suggest we turn the Holodeck off for the duration of our deployment, Sir.'

The ready room becomes silent as Captain Kirkland considers this solution. It is drastic and Draconian and something that would put the crew under tremendous stress. There has to be another solution, he thinks. Suddenly, he smiles and turns to the commander.

'Commander, order Engineering to shut down the Holodeck immediately.'

'But Sir, the crew will lose all of its entertainment. It will crush them to have the next four years of the expedition without the Holodeck. I beg you to reconsider, Captain,' retorts Commander Trevin.

'Commander, can you tell me what is in deck seven, section sixteen, level five?' asks the captain.

'Why Captain, that location is the old library. We have not used it since the late 2900 when the Holodeck Program was first commissioned and incorporated into the modern starships. Do you expect the crew to use it now?' asks commander Trevin.

'The Holodeck Program can only fill a part of the human consciousness with familiarity and a sense of what we programmed it to do. It can only interact with the human participant. It cannot express a feeling, but a writer through his stories can. The library holds a world ready for us to 'live in' not just interact with. So, whether the crew uses a physical book or a tablet, or an e-reader, the crew member will transport themself to a world they can 'feel.' So, Chaplain Bell, you will now have a love of books instead of Meggie Cleary. Commander Trevin, we now will go back to the future where it all began. In books!'

'Dismissed,' says the captain, as he wonders what he will read tonight.

A LOVELY HUMAN BEING

Technology has finally arrived at my doorstep, and I have opened the door to a new world. For the past fifty-five years, I have remained a dedicated bachelor. My entire attitude towards the other sex have been that when the right woman comes along, I would find her. But that strategy has proven quite elusive in attaining my goal as a partner. So last night I went out on a limb and joined TINDER.

TINDER is a new sensation for young and older people. It is a social network program that provides a lot of benefits for its users. For example, you can eliminate all the small talk that is necessary to form a healthy relationship; It lets you meet people outside your social circle. It boosts your ego by hoping to find a beautiful individual of the opposite sex (or same sex if that is the way you lean to), and it allows you to go up your social ladder by trying to go out with a partner that is way, and I mean way out of your league. Finally, it allows me to reduce my chances of texting my old girlfriends if I ever had one before.

With all these advantages, I decide it is time for Paolo Sergio Tomas O'Connor, yours truly, to venture into the world of TINDER and see what life offers.

Imagine the possibilities, you swipe one way, and you have forsaken that person to the limbo of uncertainty, but you swipe in the right direction, and you might find your true love. Isn't technology just fantastic, I ask you.

So, it is now Wednesday evening, and I sit in the comfort of my lounge in my favourite underwear with the TV on 7Mate watching *'Blokesworld,'* and my attention is on my phone as I begin my journey.

After setting up my honest profile, the screen fills up with a cascade of photographs of women in all shapes, sizes, colours, and nationalities. Goodness, I have entered a buffet world of dating. After carefully reading all the instructions on which is the correct way to swipe to connect with a person (right) and not to connect with another (left), I start my voyage into the dating world of TINDER.

Thinking of my profile and photograph, I try to see based on the photo and short profile if this candidate or that candidate would be open to a potential meet up with me. Now I am no catch per se, but at fifty-five years of age, I have a decent six-figure salary (low figures by the way), a reasonably shaped body, and I have all my natural hair, so that has to be a plus.

TINDER must be a numbers game, and I am not that type, so I look for about thirty minutes and do a lot of swipes left until I see the picture of a plain looking woman. There is something in her eyes, and I love her name

'Betty K. Baylor,' just like the actor. So, I held the phone in my hand, read her profile, and saw that we had several things in common and I posted my first attempt at connecting on TINDER to a total stranger.

She had this dress on with white polka dots on a blue background, so I send her a message without thinking: 'My mother has a dress just like yours,' and I send it before I realise what I just typed and know at that moment that my first shot in TINDER was a blank, for sure.

To my surprise, in precisely twelve minutes I get a response from 'Betty K. Baylor' saying that was a lovely thing to say with one of those cute yellow face things or whatever they are called attached. My heart jumped. I had a response on my opening try, so my first thought was, 'is something wrong with her?'.

So, for the next hour we exchange messages about everything and about nothing, making each other laugh and having a wonderful time. It is early in the piece and with every minute that passes, I get a bit more comfortable but I still cannot bring myself to ask her out so I ask if I can continue to text her in the next day or so and she says yes without hesitation.

Over the next few weeks, we continue our conversations. Sometimes we would speak late into the evenings, other times we speak in the middle of the afternoon. There is no pattern for when we speak; we just enjoy our time together as strange as it may sound. But somehow, we get to know each other more intimately than either of us ever thought we would.

The decisive moment arrived on a Thursday evening in November 2001 when I told 'Betty K. Baylor' I was in Sydney for some work and would love to meet her at the local watering hole of the Westin Hotel in Sydney. My heart beat hard and hard, thinking I might have pushed her away from me since it was over five minutes before she replied. She replies saying she would be more than happy to meet up with me but would like to do so on Sunday afternoon, if possible, to which I reply, 'not an issue'. I will wait for her as long as needed; I think to myself. 'Betty K. Baylor' told me she is eager to meet me but that for the next few days she would be not able to be in contact but at 5 PM on Sunday she would be in the lobby of the Westin Hotel in Sydney waiting for me.

So, we made it a date. My first date in TINDER after eight months of messaging with this one lovely human being. I give her my real mobile number this time, making an excuse that I will change providers in the next day or so which she gladly took with no hesitation since TINDER will connect us using location-based technology, so it should be easy to find each other. I asked Betty for her number and she provides it, again, without hesitation. A good sign I think to myself.

The rest of the week has been the slowest week in my life. I mean, how is it possible for the time to even go slower than when you are at work, but it did. I do not help myself either by looking at the clock one hundred times a day, so it is all my fault as well.

The weekend arrives, and all I do on Saturday is to throw clothes on the bed to see what I would wear to meet Miss Betty K. Baylor. I am like a teenage girl getting ready for the social prom in high school. I mean, how badly do I have it, and I have not even met the woman yet. What if it all is a sham? What if she is not really a woman, but some SOB playing a sick joke on me, and he and his friends are sitting in the Westin Hotel lobby waiting for me to laugh me out of the hotel lobby?

I need to stop overthinking. There is no way that this is a hoax. She 'speaks' like a lady, she 'feels' like a lady, she has to be a lady, I convince myself. But I also have a small shot of bourbon to ease my anxiety.

Sunday morning, the day is blossoming, so it feels like a good omen. I try to maintain composure all day long. I have my breakfast, read the entire Sydney Gazette, front to back, including the sports section, of which I am not much of a fan. I prepare a light lunch, shower and head to the train station to catch the next train to Wynyard station, the closest to the Westin Hotel in Sydney.

A short walk from the station to the hotel and I arrive at 4:40 PM, early I think, which is good. If this is a prank, I can realise it as I walk around the lobby, but I do not see any suspicious looking person or group of persons, so maybe everything is just in my head. I settle into the chair in the lobby and check my watch. 4:55 PM, almost time. I remind myself that I know some women lack punctuality, which they wear as a badge of honour, and I should not expect to see her at the agreed upon time.

As time passed, my world shook a bit because 5 PM had arrives and passes and no 'Betty K. Baylor'. At 5:20 PM, my phone rings, and a male voice asks; 'Is this Paolo?'.

Here it comes, the bomb I have been expecting, and I am going to be devastated, but I swallow my heart and answer; 'Yes, it is. Who is this speaking? How did you get my number?'

'This is James Haldon, Miss Baylor's press agent, and I am calling you to let you know Miss Baylor is on her way down from her penthouse suite at the hotel and that she apologies for her delay. Her plane landed late in Sydney this morning, and she is running late. She will be down in ten minutes. Please wait in the lobby bar for her, and she will be there shortly. Thank you.' and he hangs up.

'What was that?' I think to myself as I stare at my phone. Was this for real? No way, it has to be the Candid Camera show in action as I look around quickly for any signs of a camera or cameras, but nothing like a camera appears anywhere. I am stupefied.

Like a zombie, I walk over to the Lobby Bar (yes that is the actual name of the bar), and I sit down, and order a triple bourbon on the rocks with a shot of tequila chaser. If this is a joke, I am going home with the biggest hangover I can get, but before I can have the first taste of the bourbon, Betty K. Baylor walks up to me and says: 'Hi Paolo, finally we meet!'

Betty motions to the server to make it the same and sits next to me and continues her conversation: 'Sorry to keep you waiting but my plane was late, and it made me late for all my engagements here, then I had a nap and overslept. I am so sorry to keep you waiting past our appointment time.'

You know how wallabies look like when he or she gets caught by the Ute's headlights? Well, that is me. Here I am sitting with Betty K. Baylor, the actress and people are noticing her and asking for autographs and photos. Out of nowhere a trio of huge guys appear and start shooing them away, and we are alone again. Still, I am sitting there with my gaping mouth, unable to speak.

'Now Paolo, please speak, please do not tell me I upset you?'

'No, no,' I said, 'you are THE Betty K. Baylor, but the picture is someone else I am confused.'

Betty answer: 'I am sorry for that. The photo is of my mother, we look a lot alike, and I love that dress of hers so I used her photo when she was younger. You may, or may not, be aware that I have been unlucky in finding someone so I thought I give TINDER a chance and guess what, I found you, Paolo!'

Our meeting continues into the early evening, where we proceed to the Mosaic Restaurant for an elegant dinner featuring modern Australian cuisine which is creatively prepared with a refined touch and attention to detail and a delight to eat.

Having finished our meal, I pay by the way, and we hear the pianist at the bar start a lovely melody and we continue with the best evening of my life, the best first date ever in TINDER but I needed to ask her one question and after two Harvey Bristol cream sherries, my voice gather its strength asked: 'Betty, are we for real?'

Her deep eyes looked at me, her red lips moist and inviting moved a bit and she answered: 'Only if you will have me.'

I have never seen the Presidential Suite at the Westin Sydney and at $5,500 per night, even with my salary I would never see it, but I did that wonderful evening when I met Betty K. Baylor.

On Monday morning, I go to work straight from the hotel, resign from my job. I call my real estate agent and say that he could put the apartment in North Sydney up for sale in one week. I also ask him to hire a crew to pack everything up, place all the furniture and apartment stuff in a rental unit for one year because I am leaving the country in a week, heading for California to get married.

He asks me to whom I was going to be wed to, and I say; 'Betty K. Baylor' and he laughs, and you know, so do I. I hang up the phone and return to the Westin Hotel, heading to the private lift, and insert the door key to find one lovely human being waiting for me.

A STAR IS MADE

One day I am minding my business in Antarctica just hanging with my friends and here comes a huge furry figure that at first, I mistake for a bear except its coat was dark not the usual white and this odd-looking figure is pointing something at me.

Next thing I know I hear this clicking sound and lots of 'Ohs' and 'Ahs' emitting from the figure and then as if by magic, this long appendage stretches out and hands me a business card: 'Mikey Lazar, Photographer to the Stars.'

OK, you read this and say to yourself: 'How did he find you in Antarctica?' Easy, I suppose, that is where I live all year long. I am comfortable here and happy mostly, but Mikey presents me with an exciting opportunity. He says to me, 'Darling, you are gorgeous! I am so glad I have discovered you! Look at your white stomach and your black head, black back, black tail and black wings. The yellowy-gold markings on the side of your head and neck sparkle like gold! Add to this your height is simply perfect. What are you, darling? About 115 centimetres? More? Less? Don't tell me; let me guess.'

Mikey continues speaking, and I do not hear him anymore. All I have is the clicking sound of his funny looking contraption and the constant lighting rays that come out of his machine. So, I ask him: 'What do you want of me?'

'You are the best-looking tuxedo-wearing individual I have ever seen. I feel I can make you into a star in the tuxedo rental business. I can pay you exceptionally well in both silverfish, krill and squid. Just name your price darling, I want you!'

I have a lot of free time until next June, so I think, why not!

'You got yourself a deal, Mikey. Where do I sign up?'

Next thing you know I am up in beautiful sunny Sydney in a place called Taronga Zoo, and I have this nice enclosure that looks so much like home that at first, I think I never left home. They give me food every day, buckets full and Mikey makes sure that another figure called a 'handler' comes in and brushes me every morning before Mikey comes in and takes photos. (I found out that is what he does with the contraption, he calls it a camera) and the constant clicking goes on and on and on for hours after hours.

So, the day arrives when Mikey says to me: 'Darling, today is the day! We will go into the central business district in Sydney to its premier store, Walter Bowes, for the annual millinery show of the spring and summer season. Think nothing but great outfits for the Melbourne Cup. All the dressed-up ladies and you will look just elegant wearing your tuxedo. You will be a champ. You will look just smashing!'

As we head down to Walter Bowes in Mikey's van, we encounter a blockade of individuals representing an organisation called IETA (Individuals for the Ethical Treatment of Animals), which make it impossible for us to get into the Walter Bowes building for the show. Mikey seems flustered, but he does not give up. Mikey thrashes about the back of the van and produces a large mink coat, which he throws over me, and we get out of the van.

We walk up to the side entrance of the Walter Bowes building trying to avoid the gaze of the IETA folks when suddenly someone yells out: 'Look, a model is wearing a minx coat!' Next thing I am covered in red liquid and is on my skin, as well. Mikey and I get into the building, but it is too late for something liquid has completely soaked us in red liquid.

Mikey and others attempt to remove the red liquid from me, but to no avail. I am ruined. My career as a tuxedo model in Sydney is over before it even started and I do not even get to meet Walter Bowes, whoever he is. Mikey shrugs his shoulders and says: 'Sorry buddy, it looks like it is the end of the road for our partnership. Your red stain is all over your back and front and is just not coming off. Your days as a tuxedo model are over.' Mikey hands me a wad of notes of all amounts and says to me: 'Book yourself on the next airplane to Antarctica. It's over.'

That is, it. I waddle out of the building looking the worse for wear, hail a taxi, and off to the airport I head to book a flight on Antarctica Air for home.

It goes to show you as I sit in my economy seat back to Antarctica that success is not measured by what you try to do but by the circumstance that is presented to you. Now covered in a red liquid, I realise that my career is not in modelling but lies in tap dancing. I do not think any of my kind has done that. Have they?

I will be the first and get discovered. The most important thing to have a desire, and I do. Next, build the connections, learn the business, and get my first movie. I have Mikey's business card, and I wonder, it is not even October, so I have seven months till mating season. I return to the airport ticket counter and book a flight to Hollywood.

As I fly to Hollywood, I wonder how hard it can be?

Look at Lassie, Old Yeller, Rin Tin and so many more who made it, and I also could be one of those lucky discoveries. Again, how hard could it be for an excellent looking penguin from Antarctica to make it to Hollywood?

ALPHABET

Arriving at school on Monday mornings is always a drag. Beckoning you is the monotonous homeroom where you see the same faces day after day, week after week, and month after month.

Can't the teachers at least switch our chairs around a bit to make life more exciting? Do not go there, I think to myself. Every time I come up with an idea and share it with a teacher, they go berserk. Finding a teacher that understands you is difficult until I meet Ms Harper.

Great, I think, a woman that understands me finally, or so I assume. Hell, I suppose she understands me, but that is not to be. I think she would at least want to hear my ideas, but that does not fly well for me.

Just at the moment when I understand she is ready to accept my proposition, Ms Harper destroys my hope. Kills my hope would be a better word to use. Little do I know Ms Harper heard all of my ideas, but she has other plans. Ms Harper decides that being a teacher requires a lot of work and has little financial benefits. Not that she does not seem to enjoy teaching, for it looks like it for many days. Or so I believe.

Perhaps my ideas of teaching differ from hers I so assume because teaching should be a passion, a career or maybe a……

Quest! Really, that is the word I was looking for what better way to describe the love of imparting knowledge on young minds than to call it a quest. Surely there must be no other measurement for a person to seek enjoyment in a career.

Today I decide that even if Ms Harper steals my idea, I will not worry. Useless word—worry—it denotes all hopelessness in one word. Vocally expressive. Worry, a wasted word making my skin feel like, like…...

Xerosis, that is the word to describe what I am feeling, a dryness of the skin which is what I am feeling when Ms Harper tells me my idea is hers now. Yes, she admits it to me she is taking my idea and using it herself and she will utilise it in the most unusual places of all; yes, you guess it, but where else than at my local zoo.

Zoo Happy Valley is the one place I always wanted my ideas to flourish, but that is not the reason for this short story, for the reason is to use each individual letter in the alphabet to start each sentence until the story reaches its end.

HASP

All the paperwork is now complete. I make sure by double-checking and triple-checking since I do not want to end up with an out-of-pocket expense. Having an elective procedure is something that you want to make sure when you go through it you have all your ducks in a row. And I make sure of that.

Never have I thought of myself as a conceited person, but at the early age of thirty-three, I have become a fully bald man. My vanity is such that I cannot see myself in the mirror, and this rattles my entire state of mind. So, I investigate what I can do to improve my mental health and decide I do a due diligent review of my health policy to see if I can maximise my benefits and I find my answer.

Medical health insurance policies in 2019 use the term 'elective' to mean a non-emergency procedure necessary to preserve a patient's health. These may be surgeries patients choose to have done as a preventative measure, because of medical diagnoses, for quality of life, or superficial reasons. My *quality of life* is shot, and I argue with the insurance company for months on this and demand that this procedure be covered in my policy. I present my request to my specialist-surgeon to perform a hair and shaft procedure (HASP) and since my doctor states that this procedure would *improve my mental health* and thus *my quality of life* the insurance company, after much consultation, agrees.

On the appointed day, everything is ready, and I will get my new head of hair.

The surgeon, the anaesthesiologist, the nurses, the operation room and of course, yours truly are ready. What can go wrong?

The operating room is chilly, and I feel the chill under my garment. I question this, and it meets me with pure amazement from the eyes hiding behind masks when I ask why I needed to be completely naked under my gown since I was having a HASP done. No one answers my question, and I do not press the issue.

I hear various voices engaging in conversation, and suddenly this white-masked bandit asks me to count backwards from one hundred. I start: 'Ninety-nine…'

As I slowly come out of my dreamlike state, I notice I am in a completely unfamiliar room from the one I initially laid in. The room looks so much different, and it has a strange 'feel', if a room can have a 'feel.'

Another white-masked bandit inches close to my face and says softly to others around him: 'He is awake. Quick get the Director.' I do not remember even speaking with a 'Director' before my HASP, so I am confused, and I try scratching my head and feel nothing: no newly installed hair follicles or shafts. They have robbed me; I realise that they have performed no HASP.

'What is going on? Why have I not been properly taken care of and why has my HASP not been performed?' I demand.

Hurrying in, several nurses bring me some articles of clothing which is a tight-fitting unisex type of uniform similar to the ones they were also wearing, and I am asked to hurry and get dressed because the 'Director' wants to speak with me the moment I wake up.

Damn right he better want to speak with me because I damn right wish to talk with him, I think as I dress into the slim uniform.

Suddenly the door to the operating room opens and in walks in the Director surrounded by five individuals in expensive suits. The Director walks straight to me, extends his hand and says to me: 'Mr Harper, I am so glad you are well. We were worried about you for so long, and we're not sure what would result from the incident.'

'Incident? What incident are you speaking about?' I yell out.

The Director speaks: 'Mr Harper, it seems on the day you were scheduled for your HASP in August 2019, there was a massive power fluctuation in the electricity grid. This power fluctuation causes the power to overload a lot of the instruments necessary to perform the HASP, and while you were connected to this equipment, a massive current of electricity passed through your entire body, giving your brain a traumatic shock, which sent you into a comatose state until today when you woke up. We have been monitoring your vital signs, and we did everything to ensure we kept you comfortable and well, and we are so happy you came back to us today.'

'Well, that is all right, Mr Director. The way you just explained it appears it was not your fault but the electricity company and while I did not get my HASP done, I am well and ready to go through the procedure whenever you can perform it.' I state.

'Well, here lies the problem, Mr Harper,' said the Director, 'You came into the operating room in August 2019, and it is now February 2249, so two-hundred and thirty years have passed. I am afraid your HASP request will not be available to you because your insurance company cannot cover any of your bills since they went bankrupt over one-hundred and twenty-five years ago. The hospital could not collect on its bill, so we have no alternative but to let you speak with our accountants and lawyers', the Director points to some expensive suited individuals, 'to let you work out a payment plan for the bill.'

'Wait a minute here.' I scream. 'You are telling me that two-hundred-thirty years have passed, and I have been in a coma? How is this possible? How could I have survived?'

One of the expensive suits inches up to me and explains; 'Mr Harper, my name is Mr Smith. It is always the intention of this hospital to provide its clients the best of service, and when the incident occurred, it did just that. For the past two-hundred-thirty years, the hospital has taken care of you, and as science and technology progressed, we adapted what we learned, and we ensure you were well, comfortable, and as you can see, all in one piece. We are pleased to see you are well and here is our bill.'

I look at the paper, Mr Smith hands me, and my eyes water but before I can say anything another suit speaks.

'Mr Harper, I am Mr Brown, and I represent your estate. You had wisely written a will back in 2013, and this will has stayed with our law practice for all these years. If you remember you asked that our company represent your estate since you had no known relatives and over the years, we found none.'

Mr Brown continues; 'Also, Mr Harper, as caretakers of your estate, we grew your savings into quite a substantial portfolio, as you can see.'

As I glance at the paper Mr Brown hands me, I am flabbergasted as to the amount that now lives in an account at the Martian International Bank of Commerce and Trade (MIBCT) as well as other smaller entities. Way more than enough to pay for the hospital bill. Before I can say anything, another suit comes up to speak, but I interrupt him.

'Thank you, Mr Brown. You have been my banker, and I appreciate what your company has done for me. Your actions have differed from other individuals standing around me.' As I glared at Mr Smith and the others standing around me.

'Mr Harper, my name is Mr White, and I represent the International Tax Office, Australia division, and I am here to give you a demand notice for past taxes because of accounts not presented in your annual taxes, as required by law. This failure by your tax representative, Mr Grey,' pointing to another suit who looks like he really does not want to be in the same room with me or anyone, 'leaves us no recourse but to demand the sum to be paid within seven business days,' as he hands me another piece of paper.

OK, I think to myself. First, there is the hospital bill, then a statement showing me I have plenty of money to pay said bill and then someone else wants tax money. What else can happen?

'Mr Harper,' speaks suit number four, 'My name is Mr Beige, and I represent the Universal Association for the benefit of Animals (UAA). Do you remember your dog, Poochy?'

Poochy, of course I remember him! My adorable great Dane that ate like a horse and destroyed my apartment but that face, how could you not love that face. 'Yes, I remember Poochy. What about him?' I answer.

'Mr Harper, in your will written in 2013 you stipulated that if you were to become unable to take care of Poochy, they should take funds from your estate and said funds were to ensure that they took care of Poochy. Now Mr Beige index fingers point to what looks like a patchy, faded old will and I read the line; '... *that Poochy remains comfortable and taken care of until I can again attend to him.*' Mr Beige speaks the moment I take my eyes off the paper. 'Based on the wording of your will, your law firm concluded you wanted Poochy to be here today.'

I am amazed. I say: 'You are telling me Poochy is here?'

'No,' answers Mr Beige, 'but your law firm interpreted your wishes that Poochy's descendants would be here to greet you when you could attend to him, so the UAA has been cloning Poochy for the past two-hundred and thirty years, and we present you both Poochy and our bill for our services.'

Suddenly the operating room door swings open and in gallivants in Poochy (or a version of him) and the darn dog recognises me and jumps on my bed. After taking a minute or two to clean myself from his saliva, I glance at the bill received from UAA, and I am floored.

There in front of me stands the Director, Mr Smith, Mr Brown, Mr White, Mr Grey, Mr Beige, and Poochy and I do a quick recap of all the paperwork I received. Bills from the hospital, bills from the International Tax Office, bills from the UAA and a plus, a statement of assets from my bankers.

It seems I am going to be OK; there is a little of money left. Then steps up suit number 5: 'Mr Harper, my name is Mr Green, and I work alone side Mr Brown who managed your estate during the period in which the incident affected you. While Mr Brown managed your estate, he did not administer our management fee. I present you with our management fee for your estate.'

The final nail in the coffin, I think to myself, but when I look at the statement containing the management fee, I wonder if I had sufficient funds for one more transaction, one more purchase, if they still exist, so I ask Mr Brown my question.

'Mr Brown, as my banker, would you know the going rate for a toupee in 2249?'

BULLDUST

Our love of travel has taken my wife and me to some most exciting places in the world. From the large cities of Europe, North, and South America, to Asia and Africa and points in-between. Our journey has always taken us to the most beautiful settings, and today's first trip to Australia is sure to complement our lifestyle.

Australia is a vast country/continent, and while large in physical size, it has a small population and only a handful of large cities. We visited Melbourne for no other reason than that my wife, Amelia, has a cousin in Melbourne, Florida and the name Melbourne, well, came into our heads.

We quickly study everything we could about Melbourne, Australia, and all its surroundings. Never trusting a conventional travel agency, we do all our research via the internet and book everything - plane tickets, accommodations and car. We allocate fourteen days to be spent in the location so that we can fully assimilate with the people and their environment.

The day arrives, and we take off from our small town airport in Brainerd, Minnesota, connecting in Minneapolis and then to Los Angeles, and finally landing in Sydney, Australia. A quick change, and we were in Melbourne by noon. Finding the car rental section, we get our compact car, and we set off to our accommodation, the Ararat.

We give thanks to Roger L. Easton, The American scientist/physicist who was the principal inventor and designer of the Global Positioning System (GPS), along with Ivan A. Getting and Bradford Parkinson for we find our hotel easily and it is a surprise. Built in the 1860s, it stands three levels high with massive windows and doors in a significant ground and has two-hundred rooms and sixteen suites. We drive up and find no one is there to valet the car, which does not make for an excellent first impression, so we park as close to the front door as possible. We leave our suitcases in the car's trunk, or should I say the boot of the car, you know when in Rome; and proceed to the front desk to register.

The place was clean but dreary at the same time. The furniture is early 1940s which when we saw the photos on the internet looked tremendous but up closely, they seem gloomy and even mouldy. In the front desk is a man I would put in the early sixties, so we approach him, introduce ourselves, and bring out our paperwork confirming our reservation.

He says hello, looks at our paperwork, sees that we prepaid for our stay, makes an imprint of our American Express card, and hands us two keys to suite 2011 and tells us our room is on the second level. We ask if there is a bellhop to get our bags; he smiles and says that no, there is no one there but him, the cook and one house cleaner during the day and at night there is the night desk manager. He points us to the elevator and gives us a little plan of the hotel and circles where the dining hall would be for the full breakfast that came with our reservation, and then he just turns and walks into the back office of the reception area. OK, I think to myself, two-hundred rooms and sixteen suites and only one house cleaner. This is going to be an experience or a catastrophe, but fingers crossed, everything will be OK.

I will not tell you that my review in Travel Advisor is going to be lengthy and I would warn other folks of this establishment. I never look at reviews since they seem to be falsified, so I know little about this hotel other than the website which I now see is exaggerated in its description of the ambiance of the place.

Suite 2011 is huge; it has to be well over two thousand square metres, which is larger than our home in Brainerd, so that is impressive. The furniture, again late 1940s, but seems sturdy, and the bed is large and clean. We unpack, wash up a bit and hit the road before dark, hoping to grab a bite to eat and return to our room before dusk settles.

The internet has given us some ideas of the area, and we find that the *Harvest Hall Café* is close to the Grampians National Park and it is less than an hour away. Plenty of time to go, eat and return. The food is marvellous, and of course, that means an excellent Travel Advisor review, but we have a bit of a disconcerting conversation with our server, a young man in his late twenties. He tells us he knows about the Ararat and relates to us it was called the Ararat Lunatic Asylum, and that he heard that over 13,000 individuals passed away within the walls and these days the abandoned mental hospital, turned hotel, seems to be haunted.

Our drive back to the hotel is solemn. We have paid for a full fourteen day stay in advance, and it clearly states that they provide no refund for any reasons so we decide that at least we can try the place tonight and make a solid decision in the morning after our breakfast. Upon arriving, we find the place totally in darkness with just a few lamps turned on. We walk to the reception desk and see the night manager; he is even older than the day manager. Our eyes connect and he nod to us, so we approach him and ask; 'Where are the rest of the guests?' He looks at us and says: 'You two are the only guests'. Then he turns and also goes into the back office.

As creepy as that statement is, we find that with such a large building with a small staff and no other guests, surely bells should have been ringing, warning us, and giving us a sign but now dusk has arrived, and we are exhausted. My wife hates to be on the road at night, so we proceed to our suite.

We quickly change and settle into the vast bed and feel a bit more comfortable and cosier and in no time my wife is snoring her head off, and I am sure I was as well.

A little after midnight, the sound of something running up and down the hall awaken us. We listen to it, and it goes on for several minutes. I get up, open the door, and there is nothing in the darkened hallway. The single light is just permitting a view of a few feet from the suite door. I climb back into bed, assure my wife everything is OK and then suddenly, we hear the same running sounds. This time we both get up from the bed, open the door, and look down the hall; nothing to be seen.

We put on the nightgowns provided by the hotel and head to the front reception and find the night manager reading a newspaper. We ask him about the noise we just heard, and he says: 'There's a legend about a former guest who used to live in the hotel a hundred years ago. On this very night, he snapped and killed a dozen men from a local logging camp that were staying in the hotel. He chopped them into pieces and fed their hearts to his favourite cat. The hotel is haunted by his…'

'Oh no!' my wife screams.

'… kitten's ghost!' the night manager states.

A seasoned tourist would have done better research; I thought we are such seasoned experts, however, after hearing this story we go back to our suite; change, repack, and dash out of the hotel in less than twelve minutes, leaving nothing but a cloud of sand gravel dust as we flee the Ararat Hotel.

We find a two-star hotel near the Grampians National Park and book in for the night. In the morning, we speak to the reception person and explain what had happened. She tells that since the Ararat Lunatic Asylum had closed in 1998, a family has purchased the place and renovated the front entrance and its reception area and has renovated one enormous suite: 2011. They advertise on the internet, but they only have this one suite. Once booked, they know no one would ever stay their entire stay, not even one night, and with a no refund policy, they are making money hand over fist each day.

'So, it is a scam!' I say.

'No, not really. We are also part of the same family, and you had no difficulty sleeping last night.' 'So where are you headed to today on your visit to Australia?'

So, we learn one thing about Australia during this visit; Australians are full of bulldust. See, we have even learned the lingo, mate!

DINGO FROM HELL

The torch hissed as I plunged it into the river and let the current sweep the light away. Then I was alone in the dark with the red-amber eyes. Staring back at me in a furious hateful manner as if it loathes me for being here in its territory looking at it as my prey. My experiences with dingoes had been a symbiotic relationship. All dingoes had individual personalities just like people did, and no two were alike.

Mostly, dingoes are a friendly lot. I had seen how adults dingos are friendly toward each other and amiable towards pups. There was an innate good feeling happening between them. This one dingo, however, had presented a problem, one that I had to resolve now.

Something had made this dingo an aggressive animal, attacking my sheep herd and venturing closer and closer into my homestead. Something had to trigger the aggressiveness in this one, and what made this one dingo special was the fact that dingoes rarely had red-amber eyes. A mature dingo's eyes vary from yellow to orange, not red ember. Losing stock was one thing, but encroachment into the homestead was another.

After flying in the council's helicopter, trying to find it during the day, I found it a waste of time. Dingoes were intelligent animals and had learnt to associate a danger with the sound. They would wait for the noise to pass, and then they would cross the open space safely. This one had been no different, so I tracked it down at night and here we were now, face to face.

A dingo could see much better than a human, especially at night so I brought the torch and lit it knowing that this at least might give me a better chance when I would find the beast. As I saw some tracks, I followed them down to the edge of the Nepean River, where I found him.

Dogs have a long history of interaction with humans for well over ten-thousand years and dogs can maintain a lasting eye-to-eye contact with a human. It turned out that dingoes were not like our domesticated friends when it came to staring at our eyes. Dogs could stare up to a minute to a human, dingoes for less than five seconds, but this one in front of me was acting more like a dog, an extremely dangerous red ember eyed dog.

As I stared back at him, I sense he would attack at any moment, so I did not hesitate. I raised my shotgun and aimed. The animal froze for a second, but then with a hellish speed, he leaped at me with its fangs aiming for my neck. I fired, and the animal fell, dead.

I left the body where it fell, but to this day I wondered if this was just a dingo or a dingo from hell.

WOULD YOU?

In the beautiful township of Happy Valley New South Wales (NSW) on Main Street is Happy Valley's *Coffer Bros*, a unique store specialising in Australian antiques. I inherited my store from my grandfather, who inherited it from his father. This generational passing of the torch only skipped my father, who died during the Korean conflict of the early 1950s after I was born. We open most nights late since a lot of our sales are by appointment.

The store has everything you can think of about Australian history ranging from furniture, jewellery, ceramics, paintings, fine art, and movie memorabilia to books. This assortment of diverse unique and exquisite items is available to anyone who comes into my store or online. A large window display shows off some magnificent furniture for sale. For example, a colonial cedar circa 1860s glazed display cabinet, full cedar construction, which can be yours for $8,000.00. Next to this piece is a Margaret Preston - Harbour Foreshore NSW c1925, valued at $25,000 to a small Zhou Xiaoping 2010 (also known as Blue and White Bottle Vase, with designs from a painting by Johnny Bulla), for a mere $4,000, so all tastes and budgets are available.

My staff is professional, well-educated and know their 'stuff,' but they are all part-time employees, so I carry most of the burden of running the store. Right where the T-section of Oxley Street and Main Street meet is where the store is situated. When drivers stop at the traffic light to turn either left or right onto Main Street, my store is in their line of vision.

After our last appointment at 8 PM tonight I bid goodnight to all my staff, and I look at my front window display, making a mental note to do some arranging the next day I lock the front door. I walk to the back of the store to switch off the main lights, leaving just a small light shining on the front display window. As I am walking to the rear of the store, just before turning on the security alarm, there is a booming crashing sound, and it feels like a car has crashed into the store, making a sound as if a bomb has gone off.

Immediately I am covered in dust, even some glass from the window display and I see all the destruction of all the items in the front window display but several other pieces of furniture and bric-à-brac as well.

As the dust settles, I can see that something has happened, though I cannot determine what. I ponder that someone has thrown in a bomb or something, but had that been the case, I would not be alive to tell this story, right?

A few seconds pass, and I hear a voice; 'Oh, I am sorry, so I must have dozed off and slammed into your store. Are you all, right?'

Curious, I can hear the voice but do not see anyone. 'Who said that?' I ask.

'Apologies, I should introduce myself. My name is Walter Griffin IV, at your service. Please call me Wally,' I still can hear the voice but can see no one. 'Where are you? Come from where you are hiding so I can see you.' I state.

'Again, my apologies, I forgot. Let me get my hat so you can see me,' replies Wally, as I come to call him from that point on.

Suddenly a little of dust flies off a section of the area where the explosion happens, and a hat appears which suddenly rises and then slowly seems to float in the air and then it tilts as if someone has used his finger to move it.

'There, I am sure you can see me now,' Wally replies.

To say that my heart is pounding out of my chest would be the cliché of the century, but where the hat floats, the voice emits itself. So, something has to be there.

'Wally, now stop this ridiculous show and present yourself,' I demand.

'Sir, my name is Walter Griffin IV, my grandfather is the Invisible Man made famous by H. G. Wells story which many thought was a work of fiction, but it was not. Over the years, my grandfather married, bore a son who also was invisible and he married, and here I am, in front of you. Well, sort of.' Wally says.

'Why did you destroy my store?' I ask.

'Sorry, as I mentioned earlier, I must have dozed off and jump the kerb and ran into your storefront.'

'Dozed off! What were you driving?' I ask.

'A beautiful red 1934 Ford Coupe with a steel body nothing short of stunning. The inside is a grey cloth interior with corvette seats. The engine is a 1962 corvette 327cu v8 with a 4-speed manual transmission. I added a 4-link rear end, air conditioning, chopped roof, sunroof, a Kenwood 6.8-inch Apple CarPlay, an Android Audio Navigation Touchscreen, a digital radio and a front drop axle which provides it with a much more aggressive looking stance. Wish you could see it.' explains Wally.

'The car is in my shop?' I ask.

'Yes, if you would be so kind as to help me push it back onto the street before people wonder what happened and the police arrive. I would be grateful.' Wally sheepishly asks.

Following his instruction, I pushed the invisible car by simply following Wally's hat and voice. He then gets into his car and says before racing off: 'Again so sorry, but I am sure you will explain this minor incident to your insurance company.'

I stand there and think to myself, 'yes, I could explain this to my insurance company, the police, and anyone that would ask me what happened, but then who would believe me?'

Would you?

FAIRNESS VERSUS JUSTICE

'I don't know how you handle this type of thing on Earth, but here on Mars, we don't let killers run free.' The Martian News quoted Sheriff Sandra Ballesteros of the Happy Valley City.

Being sheriff of the oldest settlement on Mars has a lot of positive points going for the position. First, you are the judicial system since no honest judge wants to live, work, and preside over any of the domestic, commercial, and criminal matters that arise on any of the settlements on Mars. We handle all court cases through SPOTS (Satellite Plain Old Telephone Service), a combination of hyperkinetic transmission that enables both parties to be in the same room as a hologram and thus expediting court proceedings.

Second, the Mars prosecutor handles all matters from Earth, but the laws are not earthbound laws but Mars laws. Using the following code books: *Civil Litigation 2450—2455 Volumes I—IX* by Susannah Hill-Smith. *Flight, Road, and Maritime Laws as Applied on Mars* by Thomson Kimberley. *Fundamentals of Private Martian Law* by Robert Preston, *Guidelines for the Assessment of General Damages and Personal Injury Cases on Mars* by Arthur Maxwell, *The Rules of Robots* by Hugo Paul-Carson and *Criminal Codes Application on New Martian Settlements: 2415—2495* by Virginia and Abraham Kakos among some.

Third, while on Earth the process is conventional: first they charge you with a crime, you find a lawyer to represent you who then will request bail (maybe yes and maybe no), a date is picked for the trial, and you choose a jury, go through opening statements, witness testimony, and cross-examination, closing arguments, jury instruction, jury deliberation and then the verdict is announced and the possibility of an appeal happens, the process varies a bit on Mars.

On Mars, the sheriff of the settlement handles a 'complaint.' The complaint could be a civil issue between two neighbours, fence issues, for example. Or the complaint could be a commercial issue between two businesses, faulty product delivery, again as an example and, there is a criminal complaint: burglary, B & E (break and entry), an issue between a human and an AI (we refer them as 'it', for the most part) and finally up to murder. Murder is why now you find Sheriff Ballesteros speaking with the dissenter, Mr Michael Easterbrook.

Happy Valley City sheriff's department comprises Sheriff Sandra Ballesteros, her deputy assistant, two detectives, and forty-four beat officers. The sheriff's position on Mars is unique; It acts as a 'coordinator' for the process of investigation and the judicial process at the same time.

With Michael Easterbrook, the complainant stated that Mr Easterbrook murdered her with no provocation, so Sheriff Ballesteros has apprehended Mr Easterbrook, incarcerated him, and presented him with the video sensory of the complainant, a Ms Sally Brunswick of Section Three, Level Six on the eastern section of Happy Valley City.

A sensory video presentation is what all in the sheriff's department love. It is a clear presentation extracted from the optical cortex implanted on all humans living on Mars. Humans have five basic senses: touch, sight, hearing, smell and taste and each of these senses have an implant placed into each of Mars' inhabitants when they immigrate to Mars or are born on Mars. This implant enables the police to home in on any 'complaint' presented by the complainant and saves a lot of time, costs, and it is quite efficient, unlike the process of Earth.

Ms Brunswick, as the 'complainant' (and now deceased) seeks to end the life span of Michael Easterbrook since the presumption of innocent until proven guilty does not apply on Mars. If you are caught or thought that you committed a crime, you are jailed and not set free until your day in court. Your day in court comprises the dissenter, the Earth prosecutor, following Martian laws, the Sheriff of the Section, the 'complainant' (in this case the dead Ms Brunswick) and the complainant's sight sensors.

Mr Easterbrook must prove somehow that he did not murder Ms Brunswick based on the sensory evidence presented by Sheriff Ballesteros to Mr Easterbrook.

Earth's prosecutor ensures that the evidence is on record for the court's archives and that the dissenter sees the evidence on the day or the trial. All the proceedings are by the laws and posted in the legal library in Happy Valley City.

Sheriff Ballesteros will, upon completion of the presentation of the evidence to Mr Easterbrook, turn on the 'judicial clock.'

The judicial clock sits in front of the dissenter, providing him/her/it with a thirty-minute window of presentation to contradict the evidence. If the dissenter is unable or unwilling to present sufficient evidence to the contrary, the dissenter is found guilty, handcuffed, taken to the court's cafeteria, provided with lunch and then he/she/it is taken to the execution chamber where he/she/it will be vaporised using the latest technology available to ensure a swift and painless execution.

Historical facts from Earth records show, for example, that in 2117 criminal courts completed 2,315,344,176 charges against 546,141,024 defendants. The median time between committal for trial and outcome rose from 289 days in 2013 to 376 days in 2217. This time increase has created for an immense cost for the Earth's judicial system. Further reviews show that between 2013 and 2017, the annual number of convicted offenders receiving a prison sentence rose from 1,122,459,570 to 3,324,813,042, an increase unprecedented in history. A little more than half (59%) of this growth results from increased numbers of court appearances. The rest is because of an increase in the proportion of convicted offenders being given a prison sentence. The cost of processing and placing an individual in jail averaged about $110,000 in 2017 and the cost kept rising each year.

When the United Federation of Nations approved the colonisation of Mars in 2402, it resolved its colonisers, new immigrants or natural-born Martians or any androids would not tolerate those court proceedings for criminality on Mars. The judicial system enacted the new laws to improve the liveability of Mars and to apply consistency of said laws throughout the new world and its cities like Happy Valley City.

Since the establishment of Happy Valley City in 2403, the population of Mars has reached 32,232,245 individuals according to its latest census, and the crime rate has been at 0.00012700% or forty-one dissenters all processed using the current method of law. The cost of processing and ending the life span of a dissenter is $1,326.78 or under $55,000 a year on Earth.

While Earth continues to expand into the solar system, more planets are incorporating, with minor changes, Mars laws, enabling humanity to thrive.

Are Mars laws fair as the old rules of Earth? A reporter from the Australia Morning Herald asked Sheriff Ballesteros if there was any fairness on Mars. Sheriff Ballesteros answered: 'Fairness is about people's position in society being determined by factors within their control. But on Mars justice prevails, and that is the difference.'

FOR LIFE

'All I can say is, please give me a second chance, sweetie,' I said. 'I never did this before, just this once, and I am so sorry,' I said, feeling just awful.

'Excuse me, Walter, but you are a hypocrite. After all, we have been through, this is how you treat me? How can you expect me to give you a second chance?'

As the conversation continued, my mind drifted to our first encounter. It was in the early days of spring 2015. The weather was getting a little warmer, and you could smell and enjoy those new rain showers. I did my usual thing that warm, sultry night. I was on the prowl, looking for places to visit, and enjoying my life. And then I saw her - Belinda! What a beautiful creature!

During an evening, you could see so many females just hanging around the streetlamps and they would blend, if you know what I meant. But not Belinda. I could tell she was close to her home; she seemed the kind that would not venture too far and encourage a disaster but rather be a cautious one, looking for the right mate, you could say.

With a beige/tan colour and a tint of white, she looked just as exquisite, slender and had antennae like hair made for arousal.

She looked at me, and I detected sparks fly. I was sure she felt them also, for she fluttered a bit. Every male would seek a mate to begin a life together and to complete him. Many males would look forward to having offspring, lots, if possible, thus they would help around the home nest. But I was getting ahead of my story.

'Yes, Belinda, I understand what I did was terrible,' answering her as I continued to reminisce.

My courtship with Belinda was as healthy as you could expect from any male. I had a lot of competition for Belinda. This warm evening, she seemed to be just oozing a lot of pheromones, and the males were going just bananas over her. I had to act fast if I was going to win her, claim her like my queen, and I would become her king.

I had a plan. Most plans would usually be elaborate, but mine was simple. Make myself comfortable next to Belinda, and if any other attracted male thought of getting close, well, I would wing him out of there, for sure.

What was I thinking? It felt like an hour had passed into our honeymoon, and I wanted to stray already. It felt right, but I felt awful. And this is where you now find me asking for Belinda for a second chance. Termites mate for life, but sometimes, we stray.

'So, I ask you, Belinda, can you give me a second chance and let me be your king to you, my queen?'

'Yes,' she said.

So, termites do mate for life!

GHOST WRITER

The keyboard is pouring out words after words. I stop and read. Nothing makes sense because no matter how much I focus, nothing worth placing on the paper is coming out. I decide that a brief break is required, so I use the delete button and backspace key and leave a blank page on my word processor. I close the computer screen and head off for some fresh air.

My success as a writer has been limited. One short story published and a multitude of rejections, but I know I would not make a living out of this career right away. The thought of success is always present, but goodness, does it have to be so hard?

Having an author in the family makes my writing come under more pressure. My late maternal grandfather was a wonderful person, a fantastic grandfather and an excellent writer of novels and poetry. As I walk around my backyard, I remember all those afternoons on his lap as he used his old Smith Corona typewriter to present his thoughts to the paper. I gleefully remember him telling me to 'pound the keys' and help him in his works. The words just seemed to flow from his fingers onto the page. He made it look so easy, and I grew up wanting to be just like him. I glance at my watch and notice that I have been wandering around my backyard for over 20 minutes and I need to get some work done, even if it means just writing the first sentence on a page.

I head back to sit in front of my computer and notice the screen is on, as I settle in by adjusting the desk lamp and moving my notebook around a bit. I look at the computer screen and find the blank page I left is no longer empty but filled with words - many words.

Glancing at the screen, I am hypnotised, and I begin reading. The sentences flow beautifully with excellent imagery and syntax all brought together to make a first time editor's job so easy. The words do not seem to have typos, incorrect punctuation, and are all presented in the same tense.

After I read the story, I sit back and wonder about how this story has appeared on my computer. Having no answers, I reread the story. Again, I am entranced by it. It fits the mould of a perfect short story for publication. Going on the internet, I copy paste an entire paragraph hoping that my search engine will find something online to make sure that this story is not the work of anyone else. The search produces some hits, but nothing to say that this paragraph is part of any known published work by any author.

Without hesitation, I draft a quick email to my editor and submit the story as my own just in time for the next week's publication of the magazine, which had published my only short story. I decide not to write until I get a response from my editor.

Three days later I receive a quick email from my editor showing that the story was fantastic and is included in this week's magazine and that he has submitted an account payable voucher for payment for the story. He said he was anxiously waiting for another one to publish in the next issue. Would I be so kind as to supply him with a story as soon as possible?

Sitting transfixed on the email screen, I do not know what to think. I go to the magazine's website and find my story there and see that already it had over 35,000 views, and today is Thursday so that means if no one else views the story, I will receive a substantial additional payment for the number of views besides my upfront payment.

Knowing that I will receive my upfront payment today in my account, I decide to treat myself to a nice steak lunch and a couple of beers at the local pub and then return to write. I feel inspired by what has happened and head off for lunch, leaving my computer on with my word processor ready to go.

During the walk back from lunch, my mind is trying hard to gain an idea to explore on paper, but again, I am drawing a blank. Maybe stopping for a shot of an expresso will stir my little grey cells a bit. Alas, I can report that after the coffee and continuing walking home, nothing has stirred within me.

Arriving home, I sit in front of the computer and there on the screen is another story. Reading it, I see again the incredible flow of words eloquently presented to the reader in such a fashion that it reminds me of the expert strokes of a painter inspired by his/her muse while producing a work of art. Continuing to read, I fall in love with the characters, the storyline, everything. The story is perfect! Repeating my previous research for an author I find no one has created such a work of prose before and without hesitation, I shoot this story in an email to my editor.

I leave the word processor on with a blank page and step out the front of the house and sit on my front porch and watch people walk by and after 20 minutes return to my computer which again has another story ready for me to read.

Repeating this action for the next week, I end up with over forty stories. As I slowly input these stories to my editor for publication, I check the views online and see that each story grows with its readership and that my subsequent payments are becoming larger and larger, which, of course, delights me!

Then it all stops. I leave the computer on with a blank page of my word processor and return to a blank page. I repeat the action and the same result; no story, nothing but a blank page! My editor is now asking me for more and more input since the circulation of the print magazine has increased with new subscribers because of my stories and the viewer online is now over one million views a week - stories which I had not written a word of my own in over two months. And now the source of my newfound income has stopped writing. What am I to do?

As I pace in my home office, I hear the keyboard start all by itself and words spew into the word processor. A new complete story, I hope, but then I notice that it only contains a few sentences. Reading the sentences, I find a message for myself. It reads: 'How about you do some pounding of the keys now?'

HAPPY AND IN LOVE

Sally and I are in love, and in a big way. We are both eighteen years old and just completed our final year at the Happy Valley Technological College in Happy Valley, New South Wales. Now we are ready for our future together.

We have completed all our university entry exams and are just waiting for the universities to accept us into their halls of higher learning; and to celebrate while we are waiting for our answer, what is better way than a moonlight swim at Old Potter's Pond near Harrington Grove!

That is where we headed tonight — telling our parents that we were going to meet up to see a movie in nearby Happy Bay at 8:30 PM for the 8:45 PM show of 'Greta', a psychological thriller. We each are wearing our swimmers under our clothing. We get into our cars and meet in the entrance to the bushland to get to Old Potter's Pond.

As we go past the entrance, we see that there is a large playground for young children to enjoy and plenty of tables and barbecues for families to experience during a family outing. Signs are showing a variety of walking trails depending on the different ages and physical levels of the individuals wanting to enjoy this activity, with the walks ranging from two thousand metres to over three kilometres. As we reach the site of Old Potter's Pond, we find a wooden stairwell that allows us easy access to the pond. That is where we see a large white sand beach for us to sit on and absorb the beauty of the night and all the splendour that surrounds us. The night is perfect for adolescent love. With a cloudless night with a bright moon shining through all the trees, we walk hand in hand to find the perfect spot on the sandy beach, layout our blankets and remove our clothing.

Sally was wearing her beautiful yellow polka dot bikini, which I always make fun of because it reminds me of the old song by Brian Hyland made famous in 1960. Sally is looking beautiful in it, with her bright auburn hair gleaming in the moonlight. I have on what she describes as my saggy swimmers - a short but stylish fitted water blue brief made of polyester quick-drying with thousands of little yellow birds. This is the awfullest swimmer my mother bought for me two years ago, but they fit well, so I do not mind Sally making fun of me.

We lay back on our blankets and watch the stars as they seem to twinkle to the sound of a song and see the North Star. We turn and look at each other and laugh and laugh at the silly stories we tell each other. We hear a small splash of water on the pond but we continue in our conversation. We take a break and we look up to the stars, but this time we do not see the North

Star. It seemed to have disappeared, but there are no clouds to block our view. 'How strange!', we said to each other.

We decide it is time for a swim, and we walk up to the shore, and in the blue waters we see the star reflections and one dazzling spot on the pond's bottom. The light reflection is the brightest here. Sally dives beneath the surface. Then for a long moment, the pond is still until I grow nervous. When Sally surfaces, she holds aloft over her head what had to be the North Star, the wish-making star.

As Sally walks back onto the sandy beach and holds the star in her hands, she says, 'What should we wish for Danny? Our happiness for all the time?'

'No,' I say, 'let us wish for the star to return to its place in the heavens that way everyone who sees it can also wish for wonderful things.' With a quick movement of her hand, Sally throws the North Star up into the night sky, and we see it move to its point in the night sky until it reaches the spot where it has been for thousands of centuries.

We look at each other, knowing that we had done the right thing for all those individuals who are happy and in love.

HE SURE SPEAKS FUNNY

'I would like to buy a plane ticket to your furthest location to become an amphiscian,' I said, smiling at the ticket counter employee.

'Excuse me, Sir. Could you repeat your request?' answered the airline employee.

'Certainly.' I smile back at the employee. 'I would like to purchase a plane ticket to your furthest locale that will facilitate my becoming an amphiscian.'

'Sorry, Sir. Could you spell that for me?' she quipped.

'Of course,' I said. 'Which word would you like me to spell?'

'Well, Sir, I am at a loss as to the destination you wish to visit.' Was the reply.

'Oh, you must mean amphiscian?' I query.

'Yes, Sir. If you could spell it for me, I can look it up in my destination catalogue.'

I said, 'I spelled the word as it sounds, a-m-p-h-i-s-c-i-a-n. Does that help?'

'Thank you, Sir,' the airline employee said as she typed away on the keyboard and an in a moment, she says; 'Sir, there is no such destination in the world!'

'Young lady, I do not wish to be a contumelious customer, but you are in a hugger-mugger mood and unable to perform your duties. I wish to converse with someone of authority now, please.'

The airline employee looked discombobulated as she ran to a nearby stern looking individual and walked back to her station accompanied by said individual.

'Sir, this is my immediate supervisor, Ms. Blankenship. She will assist you now.'

Ms. Blankenship took over the conversation and said, 'Sir, you appear to be trying to make fools of us by asking for a plane ticket to a made-up destination. We take our jobs seriously and do not want our time to be wasted so we could help other customers with their holiday preparations.'

'Madam,' I said, 'I am looking for the furthest location your airline flies to so I can enjoy the apricity of the locale during these winter months, and you do not seem to understand me and are treating me as a beef-witted man!' I continued; 'I am a burgess of Sydney; not a blackguard, scapegrace nor a cutpurse and wish to be treated with respect in this conversation.'

Watching all this was an elderly man who moved closer to the counter and motion to Ms. Blankenship and spoke in sotto voce with her. After a few minutes, Ms. Blankenship took over the computer keyboard, typed away like a mad woman and printed out a ticket.

'Sir,' Ms. Blankenship said, 'Here is a one-way ticket to Port of Spain, Trinidad-Tobago. 15,976 kilometres away in a sunny, warm environment as you wished. The price is $2,345 for an economy ticket, but I have upgraded you to business class. Have an enjoyable stay!'

As I pay for the ticket, showing my gratitude for the upgrade, I smile and walk away, I hear the airline employee say to Ms. Blankenship; 'He sure speaks funny.'

HISTORY REPEATS ITSELF

Happy Valley, New South Wales (NSW) is a terrorised town these days, and everyone remembers Thursday, 31 October 2069. What was supposed to be an exciting time at the technology campus of the local university became a battle zone amongst the humans, the vampires and the robots.

An experiment being conducted at the Artificial Intelligence Institute branch of the NSW Western University of Technology (WUT) backfired, causing an explosion that emitted radioactive particles throughout the university campus affecting everyone there. About forty-five thousand students, professors and visitors were affected that single day. Many died but the few surviving humans were affected differently.

It affected differently each one depending on their genetic code. Some humans remained as they were humans, while others became vampires that gained an enhanced strength, while others turned into robots with greater artificial intelligence.

There was an immediate response from nearby localities' emergency units. SES, fire brigade, police and ambulances started arriving at the university to find chaos as humans battle both the vampires and the robots and the vampires fought the robots for the one source that powered all three entities: human blood and brain material.

As the emergency response units were attacked by the vampires and robots, the humans battled them and the humans muster as many emergency vehicles as possible and student vehicles and made a rush to the central business district of Happy Valley to make their last stand.

That is where you find me, Professor Margaret Ziglar, a genetic professor at WUT working in the local chemist store straddled between the sports shop and the vet. I am gathering as much medicine and supplies as possible as some of my students and some emergency respondents set up a cordon around the building preparing for what we believe will be our last stand.

Professor calls out Billy Macdonald. 'We have set up a perimeter around the store. We have enough weapons for all forty-two remaining humans, but our ammunition may only last us for three or four skirmishes between the monsters, according to Constable Williams.'

We decide not to differentiate between vampires and robots. We call them monsters to simplify our conversations, but we know they are different. We know the humans turned into vampires needed to acquire human blood to survive, and we are the last source. The robots need human brain material, to continue to sustain and expand their artificial intelligence. We only hoped to find some antidote that would reverse the radioactive particles that are absorbed into their bodies. That is why we gather to make our last stand at the local chemist store on Main Street.

When we retreated, we bring with us three bodies: an uninfected human that had died of a heart attack under the stress of the incident, one vampire and one robot. Using some surviving medical students, we conducted autopsies on them to understand how their bodies changed owing to the radiation they received during the explosion and to compare the monsters' blood cells to the unaffected dead human.

'Professor,' Melissa Campbell, one of the medical students, calls out. 'Look at these blood specimens under the microscope. Do you see the difference?' Melissa asks.

Looking at the three unique specimens under the microscopes set up in the back room of the store I can tell there are both differences and similarities in the sample cells extracted from the vampire, the robot and the test human. Red cells contain a unique protein called haemoglobin, which helps carry oxygen from the lungs to the rest of the body and then returns carbon dioxide from the body to the lungs so that it can be exhaled. Both the vampires and humans had them but not the robots. All three blood samples had neuron cells which differ from other cells because the neurons communicate with each other through an electrochemical process. The robots and vampires, however, have one distinction besides the blood; they do not act like humans.

'Melissa, please get three brain cell samples as soon as you can for me.' Professor Ziglar asks and heads to the front of the store where Constable Williams is. 'Constable Williams, how are we holding up?'

'Well, Professor, we have the store pretty well protected. We have twenty-seven men and women on the roof, mostly the response teams that survived and a few students. You have six in the store with you working in the backroom, and the remaining nine are inside the store protecting the front entrance and back door. It is quiet outside, so we expect some activity soon but not sure if it will come from the vampires or the robots. They have different agendas.' Said Constable Williams.

'Have you been able to contact the government?' Professor Ziglar asks. 'No, all lines of communication have been severed. It looks like the explosion scattered the radiation everywhere and it is affecting other parts of New South Wales and chaos seems to be the rule of law now,' answers Constable Williams.

Melissa comes to the front of the room; 'Professor, I found the difference, quick come and see.' Both the Professor and Constable Williams rush after Melissa, who points to the three microscopes. 'There, look at the singularity in the samples. Look at what is missing in both the vampires and robots,' exclaims Melissa.

Looking into the microscopes, Professor Ziglar stares, thinks and answers aloud the answer to Melissa's' questions. 'Yes, Melissa, you are right. The human brain has three types of glia in the brain: oligodendrocytes, microglia and astrocytes. Both vampires and robots are missing microglia. That must be the answer,' excitingly states Professor Ziglar.

'OK Professor, what does that mean?' Asks Constable Williams.

'They need each to optimise brain function, and with one missing glia, the brain is looking for more. So, we have found the antidote, Constable. Please have some folks go into the pet shop and grab as many more tranquilising darts and guns as possible and then go into the sports shop and bring back all the bows and arrows they can find. Please be quick,' says Professor Ziglar.

'Melissa, can you use the extraction spanner we have to get as many of the microglia you can from the human corpse and place them in Petri dishes as soon as you can?'

For the next hour, the remaining men and women of Happy Valley work injecting into darts and the points of the arrows from the microglia cells. 'How is this going to work, Professor?' asks Melissa.

The professor looks up and says, 'Well, as soon as the microglia go into either the vampire of the robot, the individual will start getting better and slow their attack and become more human. The microglia will change the monster, meaning that the other monsters will now try to bite them and kill them, but as soon as they absorb some blood from the shot monster, they too will get the microglia they are missing and recover. This process will repeat itself from monster to monster until it cures all affected humans. They will be tired, worn out and bitten at the end, but they will be humans again, and the epidemic will stop.'

'Here they come! Both vampires and robots! They seem to have developed an attack plan together.' Yells the firefighter on the rooftop. 'Excellent!' yells back Professor Ziglar. 'Listen everyone, I know you are better at shooting with rifles, so use the air rifles first until you have exhausted the darts and then switch to the arrows. The more monsters we hit with the darts, the better.'

There must have been over three thousand monsters, all slowly approaching the store. Constable Williams thought it best to increase the firepower and had four of the indoor humans up on the roof with him. Now with thirty-one rifles poised, they waited until the monster inched closer.

At the exact moment, all thirty-two air rifles fired, and all hit a target—vampire or robot, and they did not seem affected because they kept coming forward. We lobbed now a second reload at the rear of the monster group and again all hit, but no impact.

Having just enough darts for three more tries, Constable Williams commands to hold off firing anymore. A minute passes, and the monster that is fifty metres from the front of the story halted. The first thirty monsters stop and look surprised when the other monsters attack them. 'The formula must have worked', screams Constable Williams above the monsters' roar, 'Do not fire unless they are close to us.'

Again, there is now a commotion at the rear of the monster group where the other thirty-one hit monsters are now reacting to the formula, and the other monsters also set them upon.

Professor Ziglar climbs to the roof and sees what is happening and exclaims; 'It is working, Constable, it is working! Let us watch and only fire the additional air guns if needed. Can you order the people, though, to fire the arrows as far into the monster crowd as possible? The more monsters that we infect, the faster the epidemic will stop.'

With that order, Constable Williams has the people bombard the monster with showers of arrows upon arrows until they run out of arrows. Three hundred and twelve flew, and most landed on their targets.

The monsters are upon each other increasingly aggressively and then they fall exhausted until Main Street is nothing but a blanket of bodies stacked on top of bodies and silence comes over Happy Valley.

'Now we wait, Constable Williams,' says Professor Ziglar, 'Now we wait as long as it takes to see if we have beaten this curse.'

An hour passes, and there is a moment in the front lines of the monster group. People are getting up, all beaten and bloodied but not aggressive. Some of them look up and see the humans on the top of the roof, and one of them yells out, 'What the hell are you guys doing up there?'

The rooftop humans all scream, yell, cry and wave back as more 'monsters' get up and look around Main Street in Happy Valley and wonder what happened.

With the found knowledge, Constable Williams leads a group of about one-thousand ex-vampires and robots south toward Canberra, and Melissa directs the rest north toward Newcastle and started the same process over and over, slowly eradicating the nemesis around NSW and the rest of the country.

By 2082, humans again ruled the land. Constable Williams, Professor Ziglar, and Melissa Campbell are recognised with the newly established Star of Australia medal for their efforts in eradicating the scourge that almost destroyed the country.

Back at the WSU, classes were starting and students were going about their studies and experiments when there was an explosion at the Artificial Intelligence Institute..........

HUMAN EXPERIENCE

The evening drive is always my favourite. Driving through the old Remembrance Drive in Happy Valley NSW is so delightful than using the Hume Highway. While the driving speeds varied to each highway, the scenery is something to behold when you go down Remembrance Drive.

The large and small pastures are now being covered by the evening's last rays of light, giving each field an eerie look, almost looking surreal. The early dusk has now turned into a grey and black night with not a moon in sight, which makes most of the road very treacherous. Being cautious is always a wise thing while driving down this road. But today I am in a hurry since I have done something that the local authorities would deem as illegal.

There is an immense light about one kilometre in front of me, heading straight towards my little car. I try to block the bright light with my hand, but to no avail. It is just too bright, and the light keeps getting brighter and closer.

I cannot see, and my only instinct is to swerve to the left to avoid the light, which I do, eventually hitting a wooden fence, smashing it to smatterings and stopping in the middle of a large paddock.

After the smoke and dust settles, I notice a figure walking towards me. Tall, lean with long legs and arms, and the figure keeps moving towards me. As the figure draws closer and closer, I have a good look at it. The figure is not from this world. I make sure the doors are locked, and I sat there just watching it as it watches me.

I hear in my mind: 'Hello.'

Startled, I look at the figure who just stands there in front of the driver's door, as if waiting for me to open it. I look at the figure. I cannot tell if the character is male or female. It is just non-descriptive, that is the only way I can describe it.

'Hello,' the figure says again, but my ears do not hear the word, but my mind does. What is going on?

The figure does not seem threatening, so I lower my window and say, 'Hello.' And to my surprise this time the figure says, 'Are you OK? I did not mean to make you swerve out of the road.'

This time the sound comes from what has to be his mouth, a tiny sliver one under what seems to be a nose. His enormous eyes are looking at me, intrigued.

'Who are you?' I ask.

'My name is Klaxon, and I wish to make a proposition to you today.'

'My name is James. What proposition are you speaking about?'

Klaxon replies: 'I would like for us to exchange our bodies for a week so we can each experience our worlds.'

OK, I think, not only am I speaking with a creature from another world by the name of Klaxon, but he/she/it is insane. 'No way.' I answer and start rolling my window up.

'Wait,' says Klaxon, 'think of the possibilities. You could go inside my spacecraft, do a spin around the rings of Saturn, land on the moon and walk and see the first footstep of man. The proposition has to be exciting to you, yes?' he asks.

'I could experience the joys of walking on a beach, soaking the sun's rays, eating meat pies, and having a good time at the local pub. What do you say, are you interested? It is only for a week.'

Klaxon appears sincere in his proposition and interested in how humans conduct themselves and while the idea of being in a strange body and, even more, having an alien being inside my body felt strange, the idea is taking hold of my curiosity.

'What would this exchange of bodies entail?' I asked.

'A simple transposition of genetic consciousness transferred between the host's bodies through the mind transfer modulator (MTM) inside my spacecraft. It will take less than five of your Earth minutes, and it is painless. The only side effect, if you want to call it that, you have the sniffles for the entire week.' Says Klaxon.

Well back in 1968 during that years' influenza pandemic, I survived that big case of the sniffles. I believe a little sniffle will not hamper my activities for a week.

'So, this MTM will allow us to change body, consciousness, and will we be able to do things in each other's body like you drive my car and I fly your spacecraft?'

'The total transfer means you can do what I can do, and in reverse, I can do what you can do here on Earth,' answers Klaxon.

'And it is only for a week, right? Can it go for a longer time?' I ask.

'Yes, it can go on forever, but a week is all I require, experiencing the joys of humankind. All we have to do is to agree to meet back here in a week,' answers Klaxon.

So, I agree, and I walk behind Klaxon into his spacecraft, and we use the MTM and exchanged our consciousness into each other's body. When we finish, we both smile, and we started our new 'lives' for a week. Klaxon got into my car, started it, and drove off as I got into the spacecraft and flew off.

As I am ascending into the clouds, I notice the colours of red and blue flashing lights chasing my car and the car slowing down.

These past few years have been wonderful in Klaxon's body. I have been to places I never thought existed, and I am sure Klaxon is living in the local correctional facility for robbery doing at least ten-to-twenty years. Well, he wanted to experience humankind.

IN THE JUNGLES OF VIETNAM

One of the most beautiful countries in the world is Vietnam. Its extensive coastline also includes evergreen forests. An evergreen forest includes trees such as conifers, live oak and holly in cold climates, eucalypts, beech, acacias and banksias in more temperate zones and rainforest trees in tropical zones. On the eastern edge of the Annamite Mountains, within the confines of the forest, you can find bears, primates, bats and birds roaming and close by the shoreline is of particular importance because these shorelines are the home to the nesting grounds of several endangered turtle species.

This morning, you find a young Olive Ridley sea turtle wandering the grounds of the forests, studying the many oak trees that he sees. For the rest of this story, I will call our little friend, Olive Ridley.

Vietnam has various species of these oak trees, including Quercus braianensis, Quercus xanthotricha, Quercus neglecta, Quercus macro-calyx and several others yet unidentified oaks. It is one of the many majestic oaks that our little turtle friend is studying inch by inch as he circumvents the tree's trunk.

This majestic oak tree is well over six-hundred years old and towers over eight metres eclipsing some of its cousins in the forest, and this is the tree that our little turtle has placed his full attention on.

The baby sea turtle ascends the tree trunk, using his sharp claws on her feet and stretching her tail along the tree to use it as a rudder to manoeuvre herself up towards the first branch. Each attempt ends the same way. She plummets down to the ground, and a small flume of dust rises where she has landed.

Olive Ridley continues her attempt, repeatedly; she climbs and falls. She tries again and falls. However, with each effort her claws have made an indentation on the tree trunk which enables her to climb higher each time towards her goal, the first tree branches and measly two metres high.

The effort continues for hours, but Olive Ridley reaches the first tree branch and moves on the branch to the end. She looks out into the sky and flaps her two front legs, as if they were wings, and flapping them as fast as she can, she leaps, only to fall to the ground with an enormous thump echoing in the forest.

She tries again.

She falls and tries repeatedly, every time falling.

Undeterred, Olive Ridley again climbs the tree, reaches the first branch, goes to the edge, flaps her legs, and attempts to fly and rockets to the ground.

Olive Ridley again repeats the same sequence she has done so many times and is seen by two short-tailed scimitar babblers by the name of Ricky and Lucy.

Lucy turns to Ricky: 'Sweetheart, should we tell Olive that she is adopted?'

IT'S MY NAME

My day in court finally arrived. I had spent a lot of time and money getting all my facts straight, ensuring all paperwork checked out and that I had completed all the forms. Yes, all my I's were dotted, and all my T's were crossed. Now would come the moment of my triumph and a large financial windfall.

As I sat at my table without the benefit of counsel, I saw my opponents had arrived, and they had a horde of lawyers, attorneys and barristers, all prepared to take me on. Well, I was not only ready, but I was also on the right.

The presiding judge entered, and we stood. I felt confident, powerful: yes, I will win.

You, the reader, are breaking the law today and do not know it. I have yet to sue you, but it will take me some time to find everyone that is breaking the law, but I will. I started this venture with the big boys, the instigators that had caused me to spend so much time and money, but today they would pay. Indeed, they would pay!

The judge adjusted his glasses, looked at my brief, and laughed. 'This is a mistake, right, Mr Resident?'

'No, your Honour,' I responded as I stood to show respect to the court. 'This is a serious matter that I present to the court today and these gentlemen here,' I said pointing to my opposing counsel, 'realise it is serious business what I am presenting today in your courtroom, your Honour.'

'So, you contend that these companies have used your name without compensation and are then enabling individuals across Australia to break the law?' the judge asked.

'Your Honour. It is these companies that have caused me immense emotional stress and financial angst as I try to locate all the material that the use of my name has impacted,' I related to the judge.

'And how is this a fact?' asked the judge.

'Your Honour, when I moved to Australia in 2008, I had an enormously proud and well known Hispanic name. So well known and common throughout the world, so I created myself a new personality with a unique first and last name. I applied and did all the legal paperwork myself and as you can see in early 2009 my application was approved and I started using my new, and legal, name.' I explained, holding all the paperwork in my hands to emphasise the point.

'Immediately I started receiving mail in my mailbox with my new name so I knew that all was well with the process that I had undertaken but one day

I noticed I had received a second letter addressed to me but with my neighbours' address from across the street. I researched this matter with Australia Post and found that the companies here today represented by this group of professional individuals use my legal name to address letters to the public. Mass producing these letters and thus making thousands, nay, millions of law-abiding Australians to break the law daily.' I stopped to let my presentation sink in.

'You realise I can throw this case right out the door today. Force you to pay court costs and opposing counsels' fees with this frivolous lawsuit?' pointed out the judge.

'May I ask you one question your Honour before you make that decision?' I implored.

'Of course, please ask away,' states the judge.

'Have you ever opened a letter addressed to the Current Resident before? If so, would you not say that you too have broken the law and should recuse yourself from this trial?'

So here I am now, going on my sixteen trial and I have yet to find a judge that has not broken the law either. I will get there. I am sure!

LEARNING SPANISH

The aroma permeated from the kitchen and enveloped the entire house. The cooktop had all five burners going, and each pot or pan was brewing its particular dish. Once a week my sisters, Marisa and Beatriz, and I would join my mother and visit my grandmother, and there we would see our grandmother, like an orchestra conductor, use all her burners to prepare for us our weekly lunch get-together.

One-pot contained the rice, which forms the foundation of the meal, for what is Cuban food without its rice? The second pot was simmering as the black beans softened in the broth, which contained salt, pepper, bay leaves, garlic and onions and a dab of olive oil.

The third fragrance came from the natural root boiling, the cassava, or yucca. Once it had boiled, then this soft membrane root had a delicious mixture of garlic, olive oil, lemon, and salt drizzled over it. The fourth burner had a large frying pan with a little dab of olive oil just covering the bottom of the frying pan. Here a Cuban staple, the plantain would be fried and like a painting, turned into a beautiful sweet golden yellowish colour that let the cook know they were almost ready to be served. My grandmother then would prepare the fifth pan for the most crucial part of the meal, the bistec de palomilla or butterflied beefsteak.

In Spanish, 'palomilla' means moth or butterfly, referring to how we split it in thickness to make two thin steaks of equal size. Because it was a tougher (but inexpensive) cut of meat, this makes it easier to chew, and more susceptible to being tenderised with a meat mallet, which is an essential part of the dish's preparation. Making a palomilla steak ensured that meat is available to all members of the family at last once a week.

My grandmother had now set the stage for these dishes to come together and for us to enjoy them.

The preparation of all the dishes was a family affair with my grandmother and mother speaking Spanish as they cooked and the grandchildren helping, listening to the conversation but not taking part for our grandmother spoke no English, and we spoke no Spanish, but history and food was our everyday language.

We all helped with the cooking; Marisa soaking the beans, and I remembered how much she loved running her fingers through the bowl, holding the black beans, making sure it would soften them before in the pot to be cooked.

Beatriz, being the oldest, would have the responsibility of cutting the yucca into sizes that would fit in the pot and place them inside to boil. She was accountable for the slicing of the plantains so they can go in the hot oil to create a soft and yet crispy delight and of course chopping enough garlic so we can use it in other dishes, including one for me to do.

I was the youngest, and therefore, I only had one responsibility, and that was the sixth and final burner. This burner is to remain empty until the very last moment when I would take a flat pan and after I had mixed butter, olive oil, and Beatriz's' garlic, I would brush this marvellous concoction onto Cuban bread which I would then place on the hot pan to warm and toast further flooding the kitchen with more garlic perfume.

We did this for many years until both our grandmother and mother passed away. As we all got older, and the siblings went on different paths, we could not take part in this memory each week, but we vow we would get together twice a year; Marisa, Beatriz, and I, along with our children, gather and share with them our culture and history over a beautiful meal.

It was a shame we never learned to speak Spanish, for it would have made this memory of our mother and grandmother simply perfect for all of us.

LOVELY ACORN

'Grandmother, no way in heaven's name will I be going to the dance,' I said. 'No way am I putting myself through that effort. I got better things to do on a Saturday night. Besides, there is only going to be a bunch of old ladies there, anyway.' Again, I insisted.

'First, you do not call me or my friends, old ladies. We are young, vibrant 60-year-old women who have a passion for dance and life. Besides, I lost my driver's license last week, so I need you to be my driver. Call it payback time.' My grandmother said, putting me in my place like she always does somehow.

So, I gave up on the conversation I knew was a lost cause when I could see it, and that was it. I had to be honest, my Saturday nights have been quite sucky - is that even a word, sucky? So, going out this Saturday night and watching an older woman dance would not be too bad. There would be food and drink. What could go wrong anyway, I asked myself. Besides, what twenty-two-year-old male could turn down free food and drink, right?

Saturday night arrived, and I pulled into my grandmother's driveway and honked the horn.

Nothing happened, so I turned the ignition off and walked to the front door and using my emergency key (we have one of those right?), go in and call out to my grandmother.

'I am almost ready, Bobby, give me another ten minutes, and I will come down in a jiffy.'

Well, we knew what it meant when a woman said, "ten minutes", it could cover a range of time that was beyond any man's comprehension of time. Even Stephen Hawkins could not interpret the relationship of time and space to a woman's 'be down in ten minutes!'. I am sure he gave up on any explanation years ago.

The ten minutes went by fast, and in another twenty-two minutes my grandmother came downstairs, and I had a double take. The 1960s featured some different trends. It was a decade that broke many fashion traditions, mirroring social movements during the time. The time's influence on designers and the sixties was no different. They gave us the mini skirt, culottes, go-go boots, and some more weird fashions. Add a little of pot, and everyone was high on a colourful fashion and weed.

What I saw was out of this world. My grandmother was wearing a transparent top with a boa and a mini skirt with psychedelic and to top it, go-go boots!

'How do I look, Bobby?' she asked me.

'Out of this world,' I said. It was going to be an exciting dance, for sure.

Arriving at the dance, I could hear several melodies loud and clear. Chubby Checker, the Beatles, the Monkeys and many more staples of the times were blaring away in constant succession, with many people dancing their hearts out.

'Is it not groovy, Bobby?' my grandmother uttered.

'Yes, it is, grandmother', what else could I say as I walked over to the bar to grab a drink to drown myself in after seeing all this. I know that the exciting night would turn into a long night.

As the night progressed and it got later, I continued sipping my drink at the bar. Suddenly, I felt a bump on my arm, and I turned and saw what I could only describe as a goddess. This goddess stood 1.7 metres tall, looking fabulous in her high heel with youthful energy and age-defying hourglass physique. She wore a black low-cut dress that women several decades her junior would be happy to pull off.

Her hazel eyes seemed to glow under the disco lights, while her red lips were just like rose petals. I must admit, I never laid eyes on a woman like this.

'Oh, so sorry. Did I make you spill your drink?' the goddess spoke.

'Ah, no, of course not! It was probably my fault for standing in your way.' Oh God, what a response, I was an idiot!

She threw her head back and laughed the sweetest laugh I had ever heard. Is there anything she could not do wrong?

'My name is Bobby. What is yours?' I queried.

'Sophia,' she answered. 'Nice to meet you. Are you here alone?' she asked.

OK, ok, Bobby does not panic. Think man, think. If you say you are here with your grandmother, you are going to blow this, blow it! I thought in my head.

'I am one of the dance promoters.' I lied.

'Oh, that is nice. It is quite a delightful dance, and I love the music. The music brings back to me so many memories of good and sad times. Is that not a silly thing to say?' Sophia said.

You know, when a deer sees a set of headlights, and he/she stands still in the middle of the road. Well, that was me at that moment. Each time Sophia spoke one word, I froze. I only heard the melodic voice rings out for words, and I freeze in her trance. I had never felt like this before. What was happening I did not know, and I did not care. All I knew is that I did not want this beautiful woman to step away from my side.

'Oh, hi grandmother,' I heard, and I turn around and see a new goddess, 'I see you met my grandmother.?' The new goddess questioned me.

Standing in front of me is a younger version of Sophia wearing the same dress with the same colour of eyes and a beautiful grin. Sophia smiles at me and did a little wave with her hand and walked away, leaving me.

'I am here to pick up my grandmother, and I am ready to take her home. And you?' I asked Sophia's granddaughter.

'Same my name is Sarah. What is yours?' Sarah asked.

You know, coming to this dance was not a bad idea.

'My name is Bobby,' I said and thought of the saying that the acorn does not fall far from the tree. And standing in front of me was such a lovely acorn indeed.

MAGIC

It is not usual for me to share intimate stories of my life, for I am a shy person. Living in the tiny community of Old Lyme Connecticut, population 7,016 by the last census conducted, my town has long been a popular summer resort and a well-established artists' colony. They named the town after Lyme Regis, England, and it was founded in 1855. Easy going is how you can describe my town. It never has a hectic moment until the summer, when the city floods with summer tourists enjoying our shores.

My house is on Forest Road, located very close to the Nehantic State Forest with a beautiful park filled with native Connecticut trees such as the red maple, sugar maple, and a few more, making this park my favourite to stroll with my best friend, Lulu.

Lulu is my pet, dachshund. When I rescued Lulu from the local RSPCA store, I did not know that dachshunds were bred to dig, having short legs so it can reach into burrows for badgers and other small game. This German breed is highly active and can become a nuisance digger if not stimulated; hence, my daily afternoon walks in the park near my home, Devil's Hopyard Park.

One afternoon near dusk Lulu stops and starts digging as if something has possessed her and she is unable or unwilling to stop her digging. I try to stop her by pulling on the leash to no avail and then attempt to pick her up but, for the first time, she growls at me, and I stop my attempt. Lulu cut-offs her digging and steps back, and she seems to motion to me to look by a bobbing of her head toward the hole she has dug. I look into what I thought was a small pit; I find what looks like a bone. It was 70mm high x 45mm wide with enormous eyes and had a greyish colour to it, which made me believe it is ancient.

Having seen nothing like it, I take out my handkerchief and cover it and bring it home, thinking that I need to find out what it is. I think on my way home I may call in the morning the Old Lyme-Phoebe Griffin Noyes Library in town, where I may find some answers about what this artefact may be.

The library opens at 9 AM, so I place Lulu in the grassy entrance to the library on her leash and walk into the library heading to the research section of the library with the artefact tucked into my pants pocket, still wrapped in my handkerchief. As I walk into the research area, I find the research desk information cubicle and walk towards it, where I see the back of a woman placing some books on the opposite side of the cubicle. She turns, and I freeze in place.

She is the most beautiful creature I have ever seen. Slender and tall but not too tall, she has soft red hair stressed her blue eyes. She has a pixie face like the feature that just makes her seem like she is not from this world. I walk up to her and say: 'Hi, I was wondering if you could help me with some research, please.'

OK, I know I sounded like a twelve-year-old asking the librarian for help, but I cannot help myself. She smiles at me and returns the salutation. 'But of course, that is what I am here for. How may I help you?' It sounds like angelic words to me. I dig into my pocket and bring out my handkerchief and display the artefact to her.

'My, oh my, where did you find this?' she asks.

I tell her the location and the circumstances of my finding, or rather that of Lulu's discoveries, and continue to stare at her and her beautiful pixie face. She notices my staring and smiles at me and states; 'Well I know dachshunds diggers. I have a small Cocker Spaniel at home which is very playful. Oh, may I ask; are you a member of the library?'

'What do I think to myself is a member of the library? No, I am not', I think to myself why I should be a member but then I guess I have also missed a lot by not being one. Just look at the research desk attendant.

'No, I am not. Does that impede you from helping me?' I ask.

'Of course not. It is just that I have not seen you before, and I attend most of the monthly library meetings, so I was just wondering, that is all.' Smiling as she picks up an enormous book and places it in front of me. The book has a funny title, *Tangata Whenua,* which I cannot even pronounce.

'I know what this artefact may be but to make sure this book should help us determine what this might be for sure.' She extends her hand to take hold of the artefact and our hand's touch, and I swear to you, Electricity goes through my entire body, and I do not mean the kind you feel when you rub your shoes on the carpet and get a shock, but a different type of electricity.

A few minutes of awkward silence ensues as we flip through the pages of the book, and then we find it. The artefact is a hei-tiki.

'Oh, just like I thought! It is a Māori hei-tiki.' She speaks. 'The Māori say this ornament is a fertility charm representing the human embryo and that women should wear it only. Also, the tiki is a good luck charm and is believed in giving the wearer clarity of thought and great inner knowledge. How did it get buried in Connecticut?' she wonders, looking at me with eyes that are melting into me.

'I do not know, Miss…' I mumble.

'Oh, so sorry I never introduced myself, pointing to her name tag. I am Sally. Sally Tuatini. And you are?'

'Peter Forbes, a pleasure to meet you, Ms Tuatini. What made you recognise the artefact? Have you seen many of them?'

'Why, yes, I have. My mother is Māori, and my father is a Scot. They met when they were young in Wellington, New Zealand and married and came to Connecticut to live when my father got a job offer in Harford at one of the insurance companies. I have travelled to New Zealand frequently, and I am familiar with Māori lore and Mr Forbess....'

'Please call me Peter,' I say.

'OK, Peter, I can tell you this is ancient, at least from the mid-1300s. it is old indeed, and.........'

As Sally continues to tell me all about the hei-tiki I am feeling a warmth all over me, as if I am being enveloped by an invisible warm, cosy blanket that offers me nothing but security and salvation.

'Peter, are you listing to what I am saying?' says Sally, looking at me with those beautiful blue eyes.

'Yes, of course, Sally, I heard everything you said, and I was wondering if you and I could continue this conversation over lunch at the café across from the library.' I utter out.

Sally smiles and answers; 'Of course. My lunchtime is 11:30 AM. Meet you outside then?' 'Yes,' I reply as I gather the hei-tiki and place it again in my pants pocket, thinking to myself — that is a funny place for a fertility item.

As I am holding Lulu on her leash at 11:30 AM Sally comes out and exclaims: 'This must be Lulu. What a beautiful animal. One day we can meet in the park and walk my dog, Alby. I am sure they will have fun together.' Sally quips, smiling.

'Of course,' I say as I lead Lulu and usher Sally towards the café for lunch.

Lunch is nothing extraordinary, but it smells and tastes like a feast when I am sitting with Sally. The one-hour lunch break gets extended to two-hours and then three-hours, only interrupted by the occasional visit to Lulu to make sure she has sufficient water, food and is quiet on the footpath. I take the hei-tiki out and say to Sally; 'Sally, please take this as a token of our new friendship. I hope it is not too presumptuous of me, but I was wondering if you would like to take on a movie and dinner on Friday night. The new movie *Avengers: Endgame* is playing at the Rialto. I hear it is good.' Damn it; I sound like a twelve-year-old again.

Sally grasps my hand holding the hei-tiki with both of her hands and says: 'Yes.'

As I drop Sally at the library, and as she walks in, I think I will make sure I become a member of the local library.

'Come Lulu; time to go home' as I turn to walk home and also realise that I was not too shy today. Go figure. The hei-tiki magic does work after all.

MISSY'S BOOK SHOP

There is nothing like walking around Northport in New South Wales (NSW) early on a Saturday morning. The cafes are busy with customers enjoying a breakfast meal or a cup of coffee. By 9 AM, you see some major stores open their doors for the early trade. There is always someone famous waiting to get in at *Cut Me Crazy* since it is the premier hair salon in Sydney. Both politicians and actors frequent this hair salon, as do the general populace of Northport. You also see people already crowding into the *Village Books & Stuff* where office supplies are available and unique books for purchase.

By 10 AM every store is open in Northport, and Main Street is bustling with people coming and going. Amongst all this excitement is where you find me. I am on my way to *Missy's Book Shop*, my favourite store in all of Northport. Ms Missy has been running the bookstore for over 25 years. She is a staple in the community and enjoys the many benefactors that frequent her store to buy the latest novels and some rare books that she gets for some of the most affluent collectors in the area.

Today I am after a book on magic. I got hooked on magic just by watching the weekly Penn and Teller Show on TV, and I cannot get enough of it. As far as I can tell I am at the apprentice stage which means I can do a bit of this and a little of that but nothing like a Magician or not even close to a Master and, please do not make me think, a Grand Master. To achieve a greater level, I need to apply to the Magician Independent Society of Australia (MISA) and those costs plenty of money which I do not have. So, I try to improve myself by going to bookstores and finding either manuscripts or books on magic that will help me ascend to a higher level without the extra cost.

Missy's Book Shop is small by comparison to the larger named stores, but what it lacks in size it makes up for in style. A sweet smell of books rises into your nostrils as if incense is burning in the background, giving that feeling of tranquillity that you should always find in a bookstore. Then there are the bookcases. Not your modern looking contraptions that have no backing or are pure metal. Missy's cabinets are the beautiful handmade bookcases of hardwood, mahogany timber which surrounds you in warmth as soon as you enter.

As I stroll into the area that holds the books I am looking for, I see there are some recent novels of fiction of contemporary magic. There are books on Harry Potter, books by Penn and Teller, but no books on magic that I am looking to buy. In my last trip to the US, I was fortunate to go into the Conjuring Arts Research Centre, which gave me a wealth of information where I could find the tools I need. It looks like Missy's Book Shop will not be of much help to me today, so I decide to leave.

As I head for the door, I hear a voice. 'Is there something in particular you are looking for that I may help you find? Maybe I can be of help?' says the voice.

I turn and see what has to be the oldest person in the world standing behind me. He looked familiar, but I could not place the face, so I answer him, 'No, I do not think so. You do not have what I am looking for, so thanks, anyway.'

'Maybe if you give me an idea what you are searching for, I might point you in the right direction.'

I decided, 'why not?', I got out of bed early and drove to Northport to try the bookstore. This old guy is asking me if he can help, so why waste my trip, you never know.

'Sir, maybe you can help me find what I am looking for. I heard that there is a copy of *'The Magic of Freemasonry in New South Wales'* by Alcester Powell published in 1924 somewhere in the state of NSW and I wonder if you, have it?' I asked.

'Why is such a young man as yourself looking for such a rare occult book?' asks the old man.

Well, that sounded like a condescending question to me, but I answered him. 'I am trying to improve on my magician skills so I can enter MISA. Do you know what MISA is?' I ask him.

'Yes, I do. I am a Grand Master myself. After many years of learning and practice, I reach that level and yes, I know where such a book lies,' whispered the old man. Well, this was at least promising. 'OK, Sir, where is the book?' I ask, almost sounding like I was imploring.

'The book you seek is right behind the book *Japanese Costume'* by H C. Hinkler on the shelf labelled 'Fashions of the World' you cannot miss it,' he answers me.

I turn around and go to the area where the old man pointed to, and after a little searching, I find the book close to where the old man said it would be. I flip through some pages, and I am satisfied that this book will help, so I head to the cash register to pay. Reaching the cash register I find Missy (it said so on her name label), and we smile at each other, and she says to me, 'Oh my, you found the book. I have been looking for it for well over a month. There were some queries about this book in the past few weeks and every time I went to get the book it was not there. Where did you find it?' I give her the directions of where I found the book. 'Oh, I never would have thought of looking there,' she says.

'Neither would I had it not been for your assistant, the elderly man, who pointed it out to me,' I say.

'I have no one else working here. You must be mistaken, young man,' Missy says. I looked around, and the old man is nowhere to be found, so I shrug my shoulders and say to Missy; 'Well, maybe it was a customer, but I thought he worked here since he knew the place.'

'No, that could not be, young man. You are my first customer of the day.' Missy states.

I cut the conversation short and just ask Missy to charge me for the book. I hand Missy my credit card, which increases my debt by $345.00. Missy speaks to me: 'Thank you for stopping by Mr Marshall. I thank you for supporting a small business. Bye for now and please come back.' Missy says, smiling at me as I take the receipt and walk out the door.

Having spent well over an hour at the bookstore, I decide I would grab a quick lunch at the White Sheep Pub and start perusing my book. Ordering a steak and chips with salad and a Great Northern Super Crisp beer, I settle at a small table in the corner to read my book while I wait for my meal.

I open the book cover, and then I see it; written in cursive, the inscription read: 'I dedicate this book to the greatest Grand Master in the World, Benedict Marshall.' The signature: 'Merlin'.

Over the years, I often think of that morning in Northport, NSW; a place I have not returned to in many years. Having achieved and exceeded the Grand Master title at MISA, I accepted the first and only newly established title of Majestic Master. As the ceremony finishes and people mingle, I overhear someone say to another magician: 'Marshall is so good. You would almost think he is Merlin.'

Well, Merlin, I am not, but something tells me I met him.

ABOUT THE AUTHOR

The Cuban revolution in 1959 presented José with one of his many life challenges. José was born in La Habana; Cuba and the Cuban revolution saw him get on a plane alone at eleven years of age and arrive at an orphanage in the small town of Washington, Georgia. He did not get to see his parents again until he was eighteen years old and had graduated from high school in Atlanta, Georgia.

He studied Business Administration at Georgia State University. From university, he headed into the finance world working for the First National Bank of Atlanta (now Wells Fargo) and then moved into the financial consulting world working as a project manager, travelling to many assignments in the United States, Europe and Australia.

José began his writing his debut novel after getting his feet wet in creative writing at a writers' group in Camden New South Wales, Australia. This gave him 'the bug' as he calls it and soon his mind created his first major character, Danny Monk.

Currently, José is working on an anthology of short stories based on his escapades at the orphanage and other funny life experiences.

When José is not writing you can find him sitting at the local shopping centre mall watching people and getting inspirations for his future characters.

When not in front of his computer working away, José is reading or spending time with his wife in long, leisurely walks around the Camden area.

Visit www.jfnodar.com.au or www.northportbooksellers.com.au for more information.

If you have any comments you wish to share about this book or any of my books, please email me at; info@jfnodar.com.au I will respond to you in 24 hours.

Thank you for your purchase!

José F. Nodar ©   2021